Low Key Love

Other Bella Books by Cheri Ritz

Vacation People
Love's No Joke
Let the Beat Drop

About the Author

Cheri Ritz loves a good romance, so writing some happily ever after to share with the world is a dream come true! She enjoys attending her sons' many activities, brushing up on pop culture trivia, and spending cozy weekends marathoning TV shows. She lives in a suburb of Pittsburgh, Pennsylvania with her wife, three sons, and the Sweetest Cat in the World.

Low Key Love

Cheri Ritz

BELLA
BOOKS
2022

Bella Books, Inc.
P.O. Box 10543
Tallahassee, FL 32302

First Edition - 2022

Editor: Cath Walker
Cover Designer: Heather Honeywell

ISBN: 978-1-64247-335-3

Acknowledgments

I must begin with a great big heartfelt thank you to Jessica and Linda Hill and all the fine folks at Bella Books. You are supportive, and wonderful—you're simply the best! Thank you also to my editor, Cath Walker. You made some amazing catches on this one! You have an awesome way of whipping a book into shape and my story is so much better for it.

I remain especially grateful for my Bella author family, my author friends, and the sapphic lit community. Whether it's online or IRL, your fellowship and encouragement means the world to me. I also want to thank my friends at LSH Writer Roundtable—our sessions always lead to inspiration and excitement to write and read more sapphic stories.

Thank you to my sister Jaymie who was the very first reader of this story. She told me I needed to "keep it sexy." I did so, sister.

To my boys, thank you for your patience with my writer's life and for your constant support. I owe you some major Mom Bucks.

I couldn't do any of this without the continuous support of my wife. Jaime, no one inspires me like you do. No one makes me laugh like you do. You *get* me. I love you very much.

For my wife, Jaime

CHAPTER ONE

Frankie Malone leaned back at her desk and stretched her arms above her head. How could they get away with labeling the office chair ergonomic when after sitting in it for just a couple of hours it felt like an elephant was dancing the cha-cha-cha along her spine? At twenty-nine she was too young for her body to be feeling this way. Six a.m. starts to the workday were a good way to stay ahead of her workload so she could she leave the office early to volunteer at the local LGBTQ youth center, but they made for a hell of a long day.

It was barely after eight when her assistant, Cara, peeked into her office. Her sleek, brown hair was pulled back in a low ponytail, making her blue eyes seem even bigger and brighter than usual. She was a total ray of sunshine, and Frankie's favorite coworker. "Hey, Mara is over at the café and she said she needs you to get over there ASAP."

"Ugh. I am drowning in work. I really shouldn't." Frankie pushed her keyboard out of the way and dragged another stack of papers across her desk to emphasize her point. Were the manila folders multiplying? It was taking forever to get all these old files scanned into the system. When she took the Development Director position at the Clark County Animal Shelter she imagined she would be getting more doggo and kitty playtime than the job really entailed. She stole visits to the kennels and cages as often as the paperwork would allow, but it was never quite enough. Those cuties waiting for their forever homes needed more of her attention, but she knew she had actual-job duties she was expected to perform. After six years of the same old thing there was no denying it—she was burned out. "Did she say what she needed? Is this about the video?"

Cara's eyebrows raised in blissful ignorance as she shook her head. Not only was she a great assistant, she was extremely patient with Frankie's friends regularly butting in on the workday. "She didn't say, but she looked kind of frazzled."

Frazzled? That wasn't like Mara at all. Out of everyone in their friend circle, she was probably the coolest of the bunch. Mara didn't panic, and she certainly didn't frazzle. Maybe she really did need her at the café. Frankie could take a minute out of her morning to run next door and find out. She could use a coffee anyway. "Okay, yeah. I'm just gonna run over there for a minute and make sure everything's cool. Cover for me?"

"Sure thing."

Frankie closed the second button of her official Clark County Animal Shelter logoed polo shirt as she breezed out of her office. She paused in the lobby of the shelter to scratch Singe under the chin. The twenty-two-pound tabby was perched on a cushion in the front window of the shelter where he could serve as a greeter to visitors and oversee the business. The cushion used to be located in the front window of Café Gato next door until the health department put an end to the shelter cat visitation program there. The program was one of many Frankie had instituted that had resulted in an uptick in feline adoptions. To make up for its loss, she had replaced the real-live visits with a video presentation that played on a loop in the café, featuring Singe and the other shelter animals. Not quite the same, but better than nothing.

"You hold down the fort, Singe," she cooed. "I've got to see what Auntie Mara wants next door."

What could be so important that she had to make an immediate appearance in the café? Was something wrong, or was it just some silly whim? With Mara she could never be totally sure. As much as she didn't want to be stuck at her desk, she really was busy. She needed to set some ground rules with her friends about interrupting her at work. As soon as she found out what they wanted…

Her thoughts continued to swirl as she pushed through the front door of Café Gato. While reading through the never-ending stack of animal-intake reports she had bitten her thumbnail down to the skin and the tender spot throbbed angrily. She mentally scolded herself for giving in to the bad habit. Grinning impishly, Mara met her in the café entrance.

"What is it, Mara?" Frankie quickly surveyed the café, relieved to see the rest of their circle gathered around their usual table by the front window. Everyone seemed to be accounted for and okay. The wall-mounted monitor was showing the video of the dogs and cats available for adoption. It didn't look like an emergency situation. She eyed Mara suspiciously. Something was off. "What is that look you're giving me?"

Mara glanced over her shoulder at the rest of their group before turning that million-dollar grin back to Frankie. She was holding a newspaper she'd previously hidden behind her back. Suddenly everyone in the café was on their feet holding a copy of that same newspaper in front of them too. Like a flash mob without any dancing, just an abundance of newsprint.

For a beat the world swirled around Frankie while her brain made sense of it all, but then her hand flew to her mouth as she saw the headline. About that same time Mara and the other patrons shouted the words printed there, "Thirty under thirty!"

"You made it, Frankie!" Mara enveloped her in a hug as her friends rushed over to congratulate her amid the applause of the other café patrons.

The annual "Las Vegas Thirty Under Thirty: People To Watch" article had finally been published, and Frankie was among those honored. Of course she knew she was in it—she had been interviewed for it a month before. She just hadn't had a chance to pick up a paper or check it out online in her rush to get to work early that morning. Leave it to her friends to make sure she didn't shortchange herself on celebrating her accomplishments.

"Thanks, you guys." Frankie's cheeks warmed with a mix of pride and love. The group had been there for one another through thick and thin since they had met nearly four years earlier. They were like family. She waved at the other good sports in the café who had gone along with Mara's stunt. Only Mara Antonini could persuade a shop full of people relaxing with their morning cup of joe to participate in a practical joke on a stranger. "You all are too much. Thank you."

"Come on." Mara grabbed Frankie's hand as the other customers returned to their lattes and muffins, and led her to their table. "We've got your skinny vanilla what's-it-called waiting for you and you can take Penny's seat because she has to go running back to work."

"I'm not gonna just take Penny's seat."

Penny Rothmoor was the workaholic of the group and always seemed to be occupied by her position at the Rothmoor Towers Casino, her family's business. In spite of her mostly-work-nearly-no-play ways she had a kind heart and was a vital part of their circle—the down-to-earth part that balanced her best friend Mara's wilder streak.

"No, go ahead." Penny kissed Frankie on the cheek sweetly before glaring at Mara with mock disdain. "I really do have to go running back to work."

Frankie grabbed a scone from the plate of sweets in the center of their table, but any hopes she had of settling in for a quick coffee break with her friends were quickly dashed as a flash of orange zipped by on the sidewalk out front. A screech pierced the general calm that had only just returned to the café.

"Singe is on the loose!" Maeve, the gray-haired owner of Café Gato yelled as she stared out the front door. "Frankie, you better get him!"

A glance out the large storefront window filled in the gaps in the story for Frankie. A harried mother had propped open the door to the animal shelter with her hip while she struggled to push a stroller into the building. The toddler in said stroller was clapping his hands delightedly while chanting, "Kitty, kitty, kitty!" The cat was making a great escape.

"How can a cat that damn fat move that damn fast?" Mara shook her head in between sips of hot coffee.

Mara may have felt no stress about Singe making a run for it, but Frankie needed to make sure he returned safely. Singe was a resident of the animal shelter and therefore her responsibility. She made a dash for the door. "Someone stop that cat!" Once out on the sidewalk, she squinted her eyes against the bright Las Vegas sun. The orange tip of Singe's tail waved teasingly in the air before disappearing around the corner at the end of the block. She gave chase as best she could in her espadrille wedges, yelling as she went, "Stop that cat!"

Fortunately by the time she turned the corner, someone had done just that. Singe was cradled in the toned arms of a beautiful woman. With no imminent danger of Singe making good his escape, Frankie slowed to a walking pace as she approached the duo.

The slim woman's oversized plastic sunglasses and a floppy-brimmed straw hat covered a good bit of her face. Maybe she wasn't used to the Las Vegas sun, or just very aware of protecting herself from it. Even with her face partially obscured it was still easy to see she was attractive. Her lips shimmered with a glossy sheen and were turned up into an easy smile. Even stopped in the middle of the hot sidewalk with her arms full of cat she looked completely at ease. She was gently murmuring to Singe as Frankie approached. "Where did you come from, big boy? It's okay, we'll get you back home."

In addition to the relief that had washed over Frankie, knowing Singe was safe, she had a warmth spreading through her chest at this stranger's kind tone. It was melodic—almost as if she was singing. Leave it to Singe to escape the shelter and run into the arms of a beautiful woman. *You sly cat.* Frankie, suddenly conscious of her own harried appearance after her run around the block, pushed at her springy brown curls and hoped for the best as she spoke to the woman. "You found Singe and you're being so sweet to him, he'll probably never want to go back home." She grinned and stuck out her hand. "Hi, I'm Frankie. Frankie Malone."

The stranger's eyebrows shot up above the rims of her sunglasses and she hesitated as if expecting Frankie to say something else before finally shifting the big cat in her arms to free a hand to shake. "Lily," she said simply, but her smile was warm. "Is this beautiful boy yours?"

Though her heartbeat had begun to even out from her run, Frankie's chest buzzed as she held Lily's hand a beat longer than a handshake required. "Not exactly. He's from the shelter and I'm responsible for him though. The big guy thought he'd make a great escape," Frankie said, turning on the charm. "Thanks for nabbing him before he could get too far. I owe you one."

Lily shrugged it off like she was a woman who saved the day regularly. She had some kind of X factor. Cool confidence. Magnetic pull. "He came right up to me and rubbed his head against my leg while I was peeking in the window of the bakery." She tipped her head toward the storefront.

Leave it to Singe to go for a gorgeous blonde. *Clever boy.* "Seriously, if you hadn't grabbed him I'd probably still be running through the streets of Vegas." Frankie laughed and a burst of butterflies released in her belly when Lily joined in. She wanted to keep it going. "Are you from around here, or are you in town on vacation?"

"Neither. I'm here on business." Lily continued to stroke Singe's fuzzy head. She squinted through her dark lenses at the logo on Frankie's shirt. "Are you a big fan of the Clark County Animal Shelter, or is it a coincidence that you're wearing that shirt and chasing a cat down the sidewalk?"

Frankie fiddled with her shirt buttons again. "I work there. This is the official employee uniform, I guess." Polo shirts weren't exactly her own personal style, but at least she got to dress business casual at work every day. There. One perk to the job. Her heart sank as she recalled the heap of paperwork waiting for her. She dispelled the depressing thought. She had to count her blessings where she found them and not give in to the bad vibes. For the moment she was chatting up a gorgeous woman in the Las Vegas sun. Not too shabby for a Wednesday. "Singe—that's his name—is a resident there and somehow he managed to make a run for it. One minute he was lounging in the sun in his window seat at the shelter, the next minute he was on the lam."

"He's smart, I can see it in his eyes." Lily nodded as she handed the tabby back to Frankie. "And adorable."

"If you like Singe, you should meet Mr. Magoo. He's a Maine coon who loves to shower." Frankie was inspired by the brightness in Lily's eyes at the other cat's description. A fellow cat lover for sure, but there was something more there. Those eyes sparkled with something magical and mesmerizing. Charismatic. "You should come back to the shelter with me to return him. I can give you a tour if you'd like, and you can meet some of Singe's friends. Then I'll buy you a coffee at the café next door to thank you for finding him."

Out of the corner of her eye Frankie noticed two teenage girls across the street. When she turned her head to look full-on, one was pointing at them. That was so Singe, attracting attention wherever he went. The girls started to cross the street, heading straight for them.

"I would really like that, but I'm actually late for something. A meeting." Lily's demeanor suddenly changed. Instead of their easy conversation her words now tumbled out quickly as if she were in a rush. Her gaze was fixed on the girls heading their way. She adjusted the big frames on her face, tugged on the brim of her hat, and spoke a little more quickly. "Maybe another time. I'm sorry, I really have to go. Thank you for the offer though." Lily's last words were said over her shoulder as she took off down the sidewalk in the direction opposite Café Gato.

"I didn't even get your phone number," Frankie called out after her, but it was no use. Lily was gone.

Frankie turned toward the street to show off Singe to the teenagers who had been pointing at him moments before. Any publicity was good publicity for the shelter animals. There were so many that needed permanent homes, and finding those matches was the one satisfying aspect of her role. But the girls who had been heading their way seemed to have disappeared just as quickly as Lily. Frankie shifted Singe up on her shoulder, kissed him right between his ears, and blew out a sigh. "Guess we've had enough excitement for one morning, mister. Time to get back to work."

When she returned to the café after dropping Singe at the shelter, Frankie was greeted with a big hug from the owner, Maeve. "You found Singe! Well done."

"Your coffee's gone cold." Mara was still sitting at the table by the window with Jenna. They were both scrolling through their phones, unconcerned. Apparently the two of them were fine with Frankie doing the cat chasing on her own.

"And someone ate your muffin," Jenna added with a guilty grin.

"Someone, huh?" Frankie shot her friend a knowing look.

Maeve bustled over with the coffee pot to refill their mugs. "Zig is right—we are too old for this." She sighed and plopped down in the empty chair at the table. Her gray hair struggled to escape the bun that held it back off her rosy face. Rarely did Maeve sit down on the job. Neither did her husband, Zig, for that matter. Mara joked that they were the busiest people in Las Vegas. "Girls, I have something to tell you."

The three friends all leaned in toward the older woman. When Maeve talked, they listened. Unquestioningly. She and Zig had always been good to Frankie and her circle of friends. Not only with how they'd been open to promoting the shelter to their patrons. They also had given Frankie free rein to come and go, helping herself to whatever in the café. In return she had been there as needed as well, serving coffee or even hopping behind the counter to assist on occasion. Over the years the group of friends had hosted parties, meetings, even fundraisers at Café Gato. The little coffee shop was as much a part of fiber of the friend circle as any of the women.

"The suspense is killing me here," Jenna growled and tugged nervously at the pointy peak of her midnight black fauxhawk as she broke the silence of Maeve's dramatic pause. "Spit it out."

Frankie shook her head at her friend. Jenna wasn't known for her tact, but she could be a little softer when it came to dealing with the older woman who obviously had something important to share. She smiled encouragingly. "Go ahead, Maeve. We're listening."

Maeve blew out another long sigh and waved the dish towel, usually tucked into her apron, in the air as if she were surrendering. The gesture caused Frankie's heart to sink. Something wasn't right. She braced herself for Maeve's words. "Girls, Zig and I are retiring. We're selling Café Gato."

CHAPTER TWO

Lily slid her orange King Ranch tote bag off her shoulder and took her seat at the Brayden Judah Fan Experience booth right next to Brayden himself. A quick stop in the ladies' room had given her opportunity to shove her hat and ridiculously giant sunglasses into her leather tote and shake out her blond, choppy hair. She had felt like a clown in that get-up, but it had done the trick. Well, mostly.

"You were supposed to be here fifteen minutes ago," Brayden whispered angrily as his neatly sculpted eyebrows bent down to form a deep V. He was always a little testy before a big rodeo, and the National Finals Rodeo was the biggest.

Vegas had been the home for this ultimate rodeo event since the 80s. It was ten days of cowboys, competition, and country music that drew an insanely large crowd of fans to cheer for and celebrate their favorite riders. Brayden had attended as a participant for the past five years, but this was the first time Lily had come with him.

"Sorry, Bray. I met a…cat. Anyway, I made it, didn't I?" Lily bit back the details of meeting Frankie. No sense in getting Brayden all worked up before his big moment to shine. She shifted in her chair and eyed her surroundings in the MGM conference room. Some of the riders had fancy booths with monitors and displays at the meet-and-greet session. Others, like Brayden Judah, just had banners and posters. There were a lot of cowboy hats and denim. Mostly men. Very macho. Very rodeo. "What am I even doing here?"

Brayden turned to her with a look of mock shock and awe. "Lily Lancaster, you are my oldest and dearest friend in the whole wide world." He ramped up his Tennessee twang to put on his full Southern boy charm. A definite bullshit alarm. "I need you here for moral support."

Lily and Brayden had been friends since their middle school days when he would entertain her with rope tricks and to his endless amusement, she would write him silly songs and sing at the top of her lungs. Out in her daddy's fields there was nobody to tell her to hush up, and the two could be as loud as they wanted and laugh at each other's shenanigans for hours on end. But that was over ten years ago and they both knew it wasn't why Lily was in Las Vegas at the National Finals Rodeo with him.

Lily shot him a side-eyed glare she learned years ago was an effective means of keeping Brayden in check when his ego got the best of him and he needed taking down a peg or two. Brayden was handsome enough with his close-cut blond hair that flopped over his forehead, and the light scratch of stubble on his chin, but it was the dimples when he grinned that really did the ladies in. Cute, if you were into that sort of thing.

"Okay, okay." He gave her a playful fist bump to the thigh and that bashful smile that worked with all the other girls. It seemed like Brayden left a trail of yearning hearts behind him everywhere he went along the rodeo circuit. Not that he cared about them in any way other than as an addition to his ranks of fans. "And you make me look good."

"Damn straight." She giggled at the irony of her words.

"Good one, Lil." He rolled his eyes. "Now hush, they're starting. Put a smile on that pretty face and enjoy the magic and wonder that is the annual Las Vegas National Finals Rodeo Fan Fest."

Lily really didn't give a crap about National Finals Rodeo Fan Fest, and she wasn't exactly excited to sit and watch Brayden sign autographs and flirt with his followers for the next two hours. She would much rather be working on her music, but this was part of the deal and she understood that. Sure, she was happy for Brayden all hyped up in his Wrangler jeans, plaid button-down shirt, and bolo tie. She loved the way her best friend's eyes lit up when the staff opened the ballroom doors and the rodeo fans poured in. Hell, she loved the rush that came with interacting with fans too, although no one would know from the way she had reacted when those teenagers had spotted her on the street earlier.

That was different. Lily had been midconversation with Frankie Malone when they identified her, but Frankie hadn't recognized her at all. That was new. It was nice to be seen as herself for a change. Just a woman in Las Vegas window shopping for baked goods. Or some other normal, everyday activity. If those girls had approached her right then it would have just been awkward all around. She wished she could have talked to Frankie longer, or even taken her up on her offer of coffee at the…Café Gato. She would have to remember that name—maybe she could stop by another time and run into Frankie again. It was refreshing to meet someone who wanted to talk to her solely because they liked her and not because she was—

"Lily Lancaster." Angela Dobson, manager extraordinaire who wrangled both Lily's and Brayden's careers, slid behind the table. She put her hands on Lily's shoulders, snapping her out of her Frankie reverie and bringing her back to the present. She had a way of being a sobering presence. Some might even call it a wet-blanket effect. "Are you meeting? Are you greeting? Are you standing by your man?"

Lily sucked in a deep breath and pasted a smile on her lips. She loved Brayden, but she wasn't only in Las Vegas to be his arm candy, and he sure as hell wasn't *her man*. She had her own career to promote. But Fan Fest was Bray's moment, and Lily was well aware that playing nice there was part of Angela's plan for her career too. "Yes, Bray and I are having an absolute blast."

"Wonderful!" Angela's voice was total saccharine—sweet but fake. Or at least it was, until she leaned in close enough that only Lily could hear her. "Move your chair closer to Brayden. Touch him every once and a while—tenderly—make sure people see you doing it. And get your head out of the clouds and engage with the crowd. There's no reason Brayden's fans can't be your fans too. Country music and rodeo go hand in hand. Win them over. Got it?"

"Got it," Lily answered dutifully as she scooted her chair closer to the hunky cowboy and made eye contact with the next rodeo fan in line, but Angela had already breezed past Brayden and was on her way across the ballroom floor.

She had been the victim of drive-by managing. Such was the life of a rising star.

CHAPTER THREE

"The bar is the Drinkmoor, the comedy club is the Laffmoor." Angela's sharp features were fixed in an ironic grimace as she pushed the cocktail napkin with the bar's insignia on it toward Lily. After the rodeo-fan experience and to unwind and relax for a bit, the women had headed back to the casino where they were staying. As much as Angela ever relaxed anyway. In the nearly three years Lily had been working with her, Angela almost always had her mind on business. This was one of those rare moments where her omnipresent tablet in hand had been replaced by a wineglass. She took a sip of her cabernet and rolled her eyes. "Are these people for real?"

As best as Lily could tell based on the twenty-four or so hours she had been in town, everything in Las Vegas was over the top or ridiculously attention-grabbing. The bigger the gimmick, the better. "The casino is the *Rothmoor*," she pointed out with a shrug. Angela's brain never shut off from critique mode. Everything was fair game for her judgment. Lily tended to lean more toward the *find joy in everyday moments* type of mentality. It was part of being a country girl. She'd attempted to let that perspective rub off on her manager, but to no avail. "They're working a theme. I think it's funny. It's like a pun."

"Puns are the lowest form of humor." Angela pressed her wine-stained mouth into a straight line indicating she was not amused. Her dark hair had previously been pulled up in a strict bun, but when the women sat down to have a drink she had let it loose to brush her shoulders. Somehow even with the style change it still looked perfect. That was the best way to describe Angela's appearance—flawless. Of course she expected those she managed to abide by that mantra as well. Best face forward all the time. No excuses. She pursed her highly glossed lips for a moment before continuing, "By the way, I was supposed to tell you if you want to see the show at the Laffmoor, just call the concierge. They'll comp you tickets. I've heard their headliner is pretty damn funny."

Lily took a sip of her beer directly from the bottle. She recalled seeing something about the casino's comedy club on the hotel's closed-circuit television channel and the preview of their headliner's set did strike her as her type of humor—dry wit delivered with a sexy smirk, but before she could even open her mouth to say as much, the women were interrupted by a deep male voice approaching from behind.

"Excuse me, miss. I'm sorry to bother you."

Lily knew the drill and shifted into celebrity mode. She'd been approached by fans about a dozen times already that afternoon while she and Angela had gone over to check out the accommodations at the Amphitheater where her concert was booked for the following week. She put on a big, down-home, friendly girl-next-door smile and turned to face the man with the voice. It turned out to be three men—strength in numbers perhaps—all tipping their cowboy hats at her like their mamas taught them to do and grinning like fools. Their expressions weren't unlike the one Brayden used when he was trying to lay the country-boy charm on thick. Like Bray's effort, their attempts didn't have the expected effect on Lily either, but she had a job to do nonetheless. "Hey, boys. Are you in town for the rodeo too?"

"Well, dang it all! It's really you, Lily Lancaster." The leader of the pack spoke up. "I'm Cal and these are my friends, Jimmy and Ty. It's...an honor to meet you."

Lily reached out and took Cal's hand in her own before shaking the other guys' in turn. If their hefty belt buckles and expensive-looking hats were any indication the handsome, broad-shouldered men were in town for the rodeo. "The pleasure is mine, Cal, Jimmy, and Ty. It was sweet of you to come over and say hello. Where are y'all from?"

The group talked enthusiastically about their small town in Nebraska just outside of Omaha and Lily listened and smiled. She truly did enjoy meeting fans. It was always fun to talk to people who loved music as much as she did, and when the topic turned to it the guys had a lot to say about that too. All the while Angela nodded approvingly in the background and sipped her cabernet.

"Can I buy you another beer?" Cal asked when he finished telling her about the playlist he had made for the friends' otherwise uneventful flight to Las Vegas.

"Oh no," Ty insisted. "Let me buy the next one."

"No, me," Jimmy piped up, not to be left out of the action.

The men were practically tripping over one another to buy her a beer. It was mind-blowing to Lily whenever something like that happened. She was just a girl with a guitar who liked to make up songs and sing. The fact that people happened to enjoy them so much was icing on the cake. But she was also a girl who liked girls, and she wasn't interested in leading the guys on in believing this was anything more than a quick hello, fans or not.

"Sorry, guys." Lily shook her head like she felt as disappointed as they looked. "My manager and I were just about to head out."

On cue Angela rose from her barstool and tucked her handbag under her arm. At least that was one good point about her manager, she was always on alert. "That's correct, gentlemen. Lily has a lot of rehearsing to do this week for the big show. You're all going to her concert next Friday night, right?"

The men all stammered polite confirmations of their plans to attend before tipping their hats again and saying wistful goodbyes. Lily and Angela left the Drinkmoor without so much as a glance backward.

"You did well back there." Angela slipped into manager-lecture mode as they descended the grand curving staircase that led to the main floor of the casino. Her stilettos clicked a steady rhythm as they went along. Strong and purposeful, every step calculated and confident. "But next time you should be the one to mention your upcoming concert, okay? It's like sales—always be closing. You know that, Lily. Put it into practice."

There was no downtime as far as Angela was concerned. The show was on twenty-four seven. That was the reason Lily kept her floppy hat and giant sunglasses in her tote. She loved her fans—they were the reason she was living out her dream. But every now and again she just needed a little break. A moment to not be *on*. That was not a thing according to Angela, and Angela's way had been *the* way ever since she had taken Lily on as a client. Including, to Lily's dismay, her love life.

From the very start, Angela had sat Lily down and made it clear that it was imperative she keep any girl-crush feelings under wraps if she wanted to go big time in the country music world. Back in their early days working together, when Lily had tried to argue against those rules by citing one of her favorite songwriters, Casey Swenson, as an out lesbian who had contributed to country music, Angela had shut it down without further discussion, then actually taken her on a field trip to pound her point home. Thirty minutes over the Davidson County line they finally reached their destination. The small-town honkytonk dive bar had a flickering neon sign reading "Gobee's." Angela gave Lily strict instructions on how to conduct herself.

"The bartender is going to ask you what you want to drink," she said as their boots crunched across the gravel parking lot on their way to the entrance. "Say 'beer' or 'whiskey.' That's it."

With its sticky linoleum floor, dim cigarette-haze lighting, and beer-ad poster décor, the interior of the bar lived up to the ramshackle wooden-plank promise of its exterior. The bartender met them with a scowl of recognition.

"Angela Dobson. What the hell are you doing here?" He growled the question as he twisted the caps off their domestic beers. "You've got some fucking nerve showing your face in my bar."

"Hey, Gobee. Missed you too. We came to listen to your cousin if it's all right with you." Angela slid some bills across the bar to cover the drinks then turned her back to him, clearly not interested in any more of a reunion. The feeling seemed to be mutual. With a dingy yellow rag, Gobee grunted and went back to wiping down the bar.

That was the moment Lily noticed the one-woman act on the makeshift stage in the far corner of the room. The other patrons weren't paying her attention, but Lily was mesmerized by her sweet, soulful voice. "Oh my God, that's—"

"Casey Swenson," Angela confirmed with a smug nod. She had dragged Lily across the county line to make her point about the songwriter. "Back in the late nineties before she penned those hits you mentioned she was actually a client of mine." She shook her head and corrected herself. "A client of the agency I used to work for. She was a hell of a performer, but she insisted on being loud-and-proud out. Nobody else wanted to manage her career once she officially came out of the closet, so as the low woman on the totem pole I got the honor."

Lily took a long pull on her beer. It was evident where the story was going, but she let Angela go on regardless.

"I sure as hell didn't know what to do with her, but I gave it a whirl. She had buckets of talent, and she was pleasant enough to work with, but I struggled nonetheless. What we learned was that lesbians don't fly with the country-music crowd. I was fighting a losing battle." Angela's lips formed a bitter grimace. "So if you love performing country music and want to make it big, you'd better tamp those feelings down and lock them away somewhere deep and dark. Unless, of course, you have a cousin who owns a hole-in-the-wall watering hole who will let you play on nights they don't host karaoke for the locals."

Lily shook her head in disbelief. She'd never heard the songwriter's backstory before. "Casey's career went up in flames? But what about those hits she wrote?"

"Her hopes of being a superstar went up in flames," Angela corrected with a shrug. "She fired my ass and went on to write and sell some great songs. I'm sure she did okay for herself. She's not doing this for the money." She circled her beer bottle around the space in front of them, indicating the unappreciative dive-bar crowd. "This is purely for the love of performing. Thankfully my reputation as an agent got back on track eventually, but it was a damn rough start and not a journey I'd care to take again."

They'd stayed in the bar for a couple more songs before leaving Gobee's behind for good, but Lily had seen enough to hear Angela's message loud and clear. Her manager was speaking from experience. That was why she was so strict about her public image. Lily hadn't questioned her on the subject since. But on quiet, lonely nights the longing for someone with whom to share her life crept into her mind and settled with a dull and persistent ache in her heart.

"Lily, are you listening to me?" Angela's sharp voice snapped her back to the present. She continued expounding helpful tips for successful public appearances, but her words became background noise to Lily who spotted a familiar face in the casino lobby.

She wasn't wearing her Clark County Animal Shelter polo shirt or carrying a large orange cat, but Lily still recognized Frankie. Could it be total coincidence that a pretty woman Lily had met on the street that morning was now standing in the lobby of the hotel where she was staying? Or was Frankie actually a pushy fan who was following her? That was the kind of luck Lily had when it came to meeting fans and why she treasured her scarce downtime.

As they reached the bottom of the stairs, Angela scrolled through her phone already onto other business. "Listen, why don't we head back to my suite? We can continue this discussion and review your schedule for the week. I'll order some room service. I hope they have good salads available with real greens, fruit and nuts. Not that romaine and shredded-carrot crap."

"Oh, I don't know." Lily's full attention snapped back to Angela as she considered the prospect of spending her evening being lectured over dandelion leaves and sunflower seeds on the importance of selling her brand. Yeah, that was a hard pass. She would much rather retire to her own room, maybe order a snack or raid the minibar and find an old 90s teen flick on her tablet. Her gaze searched the lobby for an excuse to do anything other than follow Angela to her suite. "I think I'm gonna stop over at the concierge desk and see about those comedy-club tickets."

"Really?" Angela scrunched up her face with distaste and shrugging, looked up from her phone. "Whatever flips your flapjack, I guess. If you change your mind, you know where to find me." Without waiting for a response from Lily, she turned on her heel and headed for the hotel elevators.

Lily reached into her tote for her sunglasses, relieved to be out of Angela's watchful eye and to lay low for a bit, but she was a little too slow on the draw.

"Holy fuck, you're Lily Lancaster!" The over-excited slightly tipsy man slurred. Beer sloshed over the edge of his glass as he gestured animatedly at Lily.

She sucked in a deep breath and smiled at the guy. If she stayed calm and shook his hand, maybe took a selfie with him, he would probably be on his way. "Hey there." She stepped closer to him in the hope that he would keep his voice down. "It's always nice to meet a fan. Are you coming to my concert next week? It's right here in Las Vegas." There. Angela would be pleased—she even remembered to say the thing about the concert.

The guy put his beer-free hand on her shoulder and gave it an over-friendly squeeze. Lily stiffened under his touch as he ran his gaze down her body. "I love your music, babe. Hell, I love you," he boomed. "How about we go back to my room and you give me a private concert? I'll be mighty grateful and treat you real nice."

Lily tried unsuccessfully to wriggle out of his grasp. His vise grip didn't give. Should she scream for security? He was just a drunk fan and she should be able to handle the situation without drawing any more attention to herself. Her cheeks warmed with embarrassed heat and her scalp began to tingle with fight-or-flight adrenaline. As panic announced its arrival, rescue came in the way of a familiar voice.

"Lily? Are you okay?" As Frankie approached, the drunk guy finally loosened his hold on Lily's shoulder and stepped back. "Do you know this guy?"

"I was just—" the guy mumbled into his beer. "I was just saying hello. Sorry." He ducked his head. He at least had the decency to look ashamed as he slinked back off toward the casino.

"Are you okay?" Frankie repeated, placing a gentle hand on Lily's arm offering support. The difference in her gentle touch compared to the handsy fan's clumsy one was striking to Lily, and much appreciated. If Frankie hadn't noticed Lily was struggling and come over to help who knew what would have happened.

"Yeah. Thanks." She finally found her voice while Frankie's concerned gaze swept over her. "I just...I think I need some fresh air."

While Frankie led her through the automatic sliding doors out of the casino, Lily finally slipped on her sunglasses and floppy hat. That last brush with the public had her officially meet-and-greeted out for the day. She took another deep breath and blew it out willing her heart rate to return to normal.

Frankie looked her over, squinting questioningly at the floppy hat. "The Vegas sun usually isn't that much of a problem after four o'clock and it's almost six now, so you should be all right." When Lily didn't respond, she went on. "Hey, do you want to get out of here?"

Lily's mood brightened. Finally, something that sounded like a good idea. "Somewhere drunken men won't hit on me?"

Frankie smiled, causing her deep brown eyes to sparkle as she nodded and linked her elbow through Lily's. "I know just the place."

A quick cab ride later, the two women sat tucked away at a table in a dark corner of a little bar just off the Strip. The place wasn't big enough to be considered a club, but it was definitely too hip to classify as a dive. It fell somewhere charmingly in between. Lily hadn't heard of the Game of Flats bar, but based on the size of the crowd, it was a well-known spot with the locals. Or at least with the local women.

She sipped beer from her frosty mug and took in the Game of Flats ambience. A rainbow flag adorned one wall flanked by The L Word original-cast poster on one side and an Indigo Girls one on the other. The pieces were beginning to fall into place. "This is a lesbian bar, isn't it?"

"You said somewhere drunken men won't hit on you." Frankie shrugged. "No threat of that here. Although some of these gals have been known to throw back quite a few and get a little rowdy." She grinned. "My friends and I hang out here a lot. One of them, Jenna, bartends here. Her shift doesn't start for a while though."

A lesbian bar. Angela would have a fit. Regardless, Lily took off her hat and glasses and returned them to her tote. The lighting in the bar was dim enough that she could relax. The chances of being recognized seemed slim. Nobody seemed to be paying them any mind. "It's perfect."

Frankie poked her finger at the ice on her mug as if debating her next words. A flash of that concern that had graced her gaze earlier returned. "So are you in some kind of trouble, or are you just a drunk-guy magnet?"

Heat flushed Lily's cheeks again at the mention of the incident in the Rothmoor's lobby. It was embarrassing that she hadn't been able to handle that guy herself and it was weird that her new friend hadn't yet said anything about her music. If Frankie was a pushy fan who had been stalking her, she was sure putting on a damn good act. Maybe that theory had been a little off. "Do you really not know who I am?"

Frankie gave a flighty laugh as if playing along with a joke. "Of course I know who you are. You're Lily, the woman who found Singe and saved my behind." She really didn't know. Amazing.

"We're even then since you saved me from that jerk at the casino." Relief washed over Lily as she clinked her mug against

Frankie's. It had been a long time since she'd met someone who she didn't have to be "on" with. "And I guess I owe you an explanation."

"Hmmm. Let me guess," Frankie said between sips of beer. "Witness protection program? Dodging an ex? Undercover celebrity?"

"The last one."

"Wait, what? Are you serious?" Frankie reached across the table and took both of Lily's hands in her own. She searched Lily's face as if hunting for the truth there. Trying to recognize her. Sometimes it was the out-of-context thing that tripped people up, but it didn't seem like that was what was happening. She blinked her eyes as if coming up blank. Finally she surrendered with a shake of her head. "I'm sorry. Are you a celebrity? I really don't know who you are."

Lily tried to hold back her laughter, but it came out as one big guffaw which, in turn, caused Frankie to join her as she burst out in a fit of giggles. Frankie looked absolutely horrified at not knowing who Lily was and, truthfully, Lily was completely delighted that she didn't. It sure beat the alternative scenario that Frankie was some kind of stalker fan. "I'm Lily Lancaster." Not even a flicker of recognition on Frankie's face. "I'm a country singer. I sing that song that's on the radio, 'My Mama Told Me.'"

Frankie shook her head again and her dark brown curls danced around her face. "I'm so sorry. I don't follow country music. I'm sure you're very popular." She looked abashed at not being able to place her. Lily liked her all the more for it.

"I was a little too popular this afternoon." Lily sighed. "Along with the plusses of country-music stardom come some minuses."

"Alas, the price of frame." Frankie rolled her eyes, but then she slapped her palm on the table. "I can't believe I'm sitting here having a beer with a country-music star."

Lily gazed across the scarred wood table at Frankie. Something in the way her beautiful brown eyes sparkled gave Lily the sense that anything could happen when she was with her. It was the go-with-the-flow vibe that surrounded Frankie. Everything about her screamed easy breezy, from the boho chic scarf tied in her hair, to the stack of thin silver bangles on her left wrist, all the way down to her paisley-print maxi skirt. Frankie was the epitome of cool and hanging out with her made Lily want to let loose too. She decided it was pure serendipity that they'd bumped into each other again in the casino lobby, and somehow that seemed just right.

"What were you doing at the casino tonight anyway?" she asked between sips of cold beer. "Hitting the quarter slots?"

"I only play the nickel slots. I'm no high roller." Frankie laughed. "Actually, I was on my way to my friend Mara's show there. She's the headliner at the Laffmoor."

"I thought about hitting that show too." She nodded. Maybe Frankie liked a good pun too. At least it was a sign that she had a sense of humor. "Isn't your friend going to wonder what happened to you?"

"I sent her a text when we were in the cab. I told her I met someone and had a change of plans," Frankie said with a carefree shrug. "It happens. I've seen her set a million times anyway."

Lily's stomach twisted. Had Frankie blown her cover to her friend? "Wait. Did you tell her who I was?"

Frankie ran her fingers through her curls, those bangles jingling on her arm. "Lily, I didn't even know who you were."

She smacked her hand on her forehead and her ears burned with embarrassment. If she was going to let loose, she was going to have to commit to it. At least for the night. For once there was no Angela looking over her shoulder and she had a gorgeous, fun woman by her side. And she was in a lesbian bar! She may as well enjoy it. "Fair enough. But seriously, I'm just a regular girl who gets to do what she loves for a living. What about you, Frankie? Do you love what you do?"

"I love animals and I get to work with them, so I guess that's something." Frankie's face lit up. "I put together a program once with the café next door to the shelter where the cats would go visit. Patrons loved it because, let's face it, petting cats reduces stress. And the cats got to meet potential pet parents. We had more than a few adoptions based on café patrons coming over to the shelter after meeting cats there. But then the Clark County Health Department caught wind of it. Apparently there are ordinances against live animals hanging out in places where food is served, so they shut the program down. Party poopers."

"That sucks. I imagine people enjoyed the cats' visits." Lily's blue eyes were full of sympathy. "You love working with the animals at the shelter, that's clear. So what's the unspoken *but*?"

"What but?" Frankie frowned over her mug of beer.

"Your smile didn't reach your eyes until you got to the part about the cats in the café. What are you not telling me about your job at the shelter?"

Frankie blew out a long breath and sank back against her wooden chair. Despite the surrender on her face, her curly hair continued to bounce joyfully around from the motion. "The animals are great, and my coworkers are great, and the shelter is a steady job that pays the bills."

Lily raised her brows and took a long swallow of beer, refusing to speak until Frankie spat out the rest of her statement.

"*But* my position has become a lot more about administration, fundraising and begging people for donations and a lot less about the animals," she confessed with a guilty grimace. "I'm not so sure my heart is totally in it anymore. At least it hasn't been in it much lately."

"Sounds like it's time for a change," Lily said with a shrug.

"Oh no." Frankie sat back up to refill her mug from the clear plastic pitcher. "It's just a dry spell. I'll get over it."

"Come on. You deserve to find something that fulfills you, not just *pays the bills*. Is this what you went to school for?"

"Believe it or not, I have a business degree. When I went to college I didn't know what I wanted to do career-wise, but I have a mind for math. I'm good at it. My father's an accountant so I followed in his footsteps and majored in business." She sucked in a breath. "But by graduation I knew the corporate life was not for me. I did a little research and found a way to make my degree and my love of animals work together. Development Director at an animal shelter fit the bill."

"You never wanted to be a veterinarian? I would have thought that would be your go-to dream job."

Frankie shook her head. "Science was never my thing. And I love animals, but I don't want to…do things to them." Her eyes widened and her cheeks turned to pink apples. "That sounded way grosser than I intended. I mean, I don't want to help animals give birth, or give them shots, or spay or neuter them. I don't even want to take their temperature. I am happy to stick with cuddling and playing with them."

"I can understand that," she said as she set her beer mug back on the table. She'd seen enough about what went into caring for animals while growing up in the country. "But we're talking about your career here. Your *life*. Don't you want to do something that you're passionate about?"

"I don't know. Maybe." Frankie waved her hand as if to dismiss the subject. "Why are we talking about my boring job when we could be discussing the exciting life of country-music star Lily Lancaster?"

As luck would have it, the song playing on the jukebox ended right as Frankie said her name in what came across as exceptionally loud in the sudden relative quiet. A million sets of eyes turned to the women huddled at the little secluded table and Lily's forehead went cool with sweat. How many people were now spotting her with a beautiful woman in a cozy corner of a lesbian bar? How long would it take for word to get back to Angela? Lily struggled to form words with her desert-dry mouth and as she reached out a shaky hand for a much-needed sip of beer, she knocked over the half-full pitcher, showering Frankie with the amber liquid.

Frankie jumped up from her seat laughing as she brushed her hands down her damp tank top. "Was it something I said?"

"Oh my gosh!" Lily righted the empty pitcher and yanked a handful of napkins out of the spring-loaded metal dispenser. Why did she have to be such a klutz in front of a woman she wanted to impress? "I am so sorry."

If every woman in Game of Flats hadn't been staring at Lily and Frankie before, they sure were now. There she was, Lily Lancaster, blotting a gorgeous woman's chest with paper napkins in the dark nook of a lesbian bar. Angela would string her up by the belt loops of her Lucky Brand jeans. Although the way that beer-soaked tank top was clinging to Frankie's curvy figure was causing a cluster of line-dancing butterflies to do the "Boot Scootin' Boogie" in her midsection. *Hot damn.* Angela would totally kill her for that thought. She had to do something fast, before the bar crowd got out their cell phones and social media blew up.

"I'm okay, no worries." Frankie was still laughing good-naturedly as she tugged at her soggy top, giving Lily an eyeful of the lacy black bra underneath it.

The jolt of electricity that shot down between Lily's legs made up her mind. They couldn't stick around in the bar like that—Frankie soaking wet and the both of them being stared at. There was nothing but trouble ahead while they remained in public. "Frankie, can we please get out of here and go somewhere a little more private, like now?"

Frankie's eyes went wide as if surprised, but she nodded in agreement. She pulled a crumpled twenty-dollar bill out of her pocket and tossed it on the table before taking Lily's hand in hers. "You got it."

At the cute apartment complex just south of the Strip, Frankie unlocked her front door. Lily had been admiring the kidney-shaped pool lit up with underwater blue and purple lights in the common area down below Frankie's unit on the second floor. It was weird that nobody was taking advantage of it on such a gorgeous, balmy evening, but before Lily could ponder it further Frankie grabbed her hand and pulled her into the apartment.

"This is a nice place." Lily closed the door behind them. "Was that a hot tub down there too?"

"Yep. Lots of amenities in this community." Frankie yanked her wet tank top over her head exposing her entire bra this time. The black lace caught Lily's eye and that familiar flutter returned to her belly. "There's a gym and spa in the community center too. I really like it here, but there is one big downside."

Lily surveyed the room partly in an attempt to identify that downside, but mostly in an effort to keep from staring at Frankie's sexy curves. "Looks good from where I'm standing. What's not to love?"

"No pets allowed," Frankie called over her shoulder as she ducked into her bedroom. "Make yourself comfortable. I'm just gonna wash up real quick. There's beer in the fridge."

Lily dropped her tote beside the coffee table and helped herself to a bottle of beer. After the way Frankie had talked about how much she loved the animals at the shelter, Lily couldn't believe that she lived in a place that didn't allow pets. Although based on the large tank in the living room, it seemed fish didn't fall under the no-pets-allowed rule. She sipped her beer and watched the colorful little guys swim around a plastic treasure chest and weave in and out among the underwater plants. Their bright yellow, orange and blue bodies seemed full of cheer and fun as they zipped around the tank. Happy and bubbly, just like Frankie's personality. This chance meeting might be just what Lily needed to pump some fun into her stay in Las Vegas.

"I see you met the gang." Frankie returned wearing a fresh lavender V-neck tee. "And discovered how I got around the 'no pet' rule."

"Very clever."

"I would be very lonely without Willie, Shawn, Adam, Tina, and Janie to keep me company."

"Of course you named your fish." Lily grinned. Named them with people names no less, not a Bubbles or Nemo in the bunch. "But I still can't believe you live where they don't allow pets of the furry variety."

"Ah, well it's true," Frankie said with a sigh as she headed to the fridge. "That's the rule and they're very strict about it."

"So why did you move here? You love animals?"

Frankie took a long pull on her beer and regarded Lily as if considering whether to reveal the whole story. After a hard swallow she spilled it. "This was my grandmother's apartment. I was staying with her while looking for a place of my own out here when her health took a turn and she had to go into a nursing home." As she talked she filled a plate with grapes, cheese and a hunk of bread. A fantastically tactile picnic that ticked all the boxes on Lily's list for a hearty libido rev-up. Frankie continued, "I stayed here to take care of the place until she could come back home, only she never did. When she died, I'd been living here for over six months. She'd left the apartment to me, and the other residents had already gotten used to me being around, so it didn't seem like a big deal. And basically, it reminded me so much of my grandma that I just didn't want to leave." She ended the story with a brave face and a casual nod. Just as quickly as the somber expression had taken over her face it was gone again and she was smiley Frankie once more.

"I'm sorry about your grandma." Lily set a gentle hand on Frankie's shoulder, touched that she had opened up to her like that.

"Thank you. It's been four years and I miss her still." Frankie's smile faltered briefly again as she led Lily to the couch on the other side of the living room and set their snack on the coffee table in front of them. "I love it here in Resting Palms in spite of their stupid rule."

Resting Palms? There was still one part of the story Lily needed to circle back to for all the pieces to make sense. "Wait. When you said the other residents had gotten used to you being around…"

"Oh yeah." Frankie nodded solemnly. "This is a retirement community. They're all senior citizens."

Lily bit her bottom lip and studied her new friend's face to determine if she was joking, but she couldn't stop her laughter that bubbled up and came bursting out. To her relief Frankie joined in. "You're serious, aren't you?"

"Yes I am. They are sweet people and the best neighbors you could ask for." Frankie picked a grape off the bunch and popped it in her mouth. "Mr. Lawson on the opposite side of the building is an expert in extreme couponing and donates all the good deals he gets on pet supplies to the animal shelter. His wife, the retired Dr. Lawson, heads up the Fitness for Seniors program in the community center. And Mrs. Harley has her grandson come by here once a month to clean out that fish tank for me. Like I said, good people."

Lily nibbled on a cube of cheese and nodded along while Frankie told her about her neighbors. Her sweet smile made it clear that Frankie was as fond of the other residents as they seemed to be of her. Lily admired the way she seemed able to fit in anywhere she went, even as the only non-senior resident in a retirement community. This woman was something else and Lily was glad she was getting the chance to get to know her better.

"Speaking of good people, maybe you should give me your phone number in case I get cornered again by an out-of-control fan and need to be rescued." She held out her phone.

"Well, if you think you might need me," Frankie said with a grin. "I'd be happy to help any time."

While Frankie entered her digits, Lily ripped off a chunk of the crusty bread, knowing full well it would be yet another move frowned upon by Angela. Carbs were a forbidden fruit if she wanted to keep her stage body. But for some reason that warning voice in the back of her brain was fading away. She took a bite and relished the flaky goodness on her tongue. "Oh my gosh, this bread is incredible!"

"I know, right? I picked it up this morning from the bakery right down the street. I had planned to treat myself after work. Bread is my weakness," Frankie confessed as she got up to get them fresh beers. "Do you need anything else? Is that enough?"

"This is perfect, thanks." Lily kept her gaze on Frankie who was bent over digging beer bottles out of the back of her fridge. Not a bad view from where she was sitting. She should probably decline the beer and go back to her hotel room at the Rothmoor, but there was something about Frankie—something in her kind eyes and sweet smile—that made her want to stick around. Frankie gave off a friendly, comfortable vibe that reminded her of home even with the wildness of Vegas around them.

She pushed out of her mind the last wisps of that little voice whispering a warning that there a manager just waiting to discuss public-relations strategy and rodeo-event schedules, whose head would absolutely implode if she knew Lily's whereabouts. If Angela knew she was hanging out with a woman she'd just met, and gotten to know at a lesbian bar, she would be mad as hell. But when Frankie sat on the couch next to her and their thighs rubbed together, a wicked shiver worked its way up Lily's spine. A sensation so delicious, her worries about Angela's disapproval disappeared like Mama's biscuits at a family reunion. Screw it. What her manager didn't know wouldn't hurt her. She was staying put a little longer.

Frankie shifted on the couch, tucking one leg under her and bumping her knee against Lily. "Okay, so now you know my story. Tell me about you."

"You know the long and short of it." She ran her fingers along the piping on the back of the couch, unsure what Frankie would want to hear. "My career is my life."

"Then tell me about your life before your career." Frankie suddenly pulled back and narrowed her eyes. "Or were you one of those child stars and I just live so far under a rock I've missed years upon years of your fame."

Lily laughed. The light blush that rose on Frankie's cheeks made it clear she still carried some lingering embarrassment about not recognizing her. It was touching that Frankie was interested in getting to know more than just the country-music star part of her, but it also made Lily feel a little off-balance. She didn't get that a lot. Not anymore anyway. "No, it's definitely not you. I've always loved music, and I've been singing for anyone who would listen since I was old enough to talk. But my mom insisted I get a degree before I tried to go pro. 'Something to fall back on,' she called it."

"What did you study in school?"

"I have a degree in elementary education."

"You're a teacher!" Frankie clapped her hands in delight before reaching for another cube of cheese.

"I *could* be a teacher," Lily corrected. "I've never pursued it. I graduated like I promised my mama, then focused all my energy on my music like I promised myself. It took a couple years of working with my manager to get my name and music out there, but it paid off. Finally now at age twenty-four those little-girl dreams are coming true."

"You could have been a teacher of tiny humans." Frankie shook her head. "Talk about 'Schoolhouse Rock'!"

"Actually, I always pictured myself more like a Maria von Trapp."

The women stared at each other for a silent beat before they both unleashed a roar of raucous laughter.

Lily swiped at the tears under her eyes. She couldn't believe her luck to be sitting with this sexy, smart woman with whom she could laugh until she cried. She was so incredibly drawn to Frankie's joyful laughter and infectious smile and full lips. And there was no Angela looking over her shoulder to tell her what she should or shouldn't feel. Beside her recovering from their mirth, Frankie sucked in air and slapped her knee. At the touch a shiver shook Lily's core and made her nipples go rock hard. She never got a night like this, and while she had it in her grasp, she wasn't going to let it go.

Frankie had been surprised by her good fortune running into Lily in the lobby of the Rothmoor Towers Casino that afternoon, and learning Lily was a country-music star. But the biggest surprise of all was Lily's eagerness to get out of Game of Flats and go somewhere more private. She'd felt like a celebrity herself walking out of the bar with the gorgeous, not to mention famous, woman on her arm. The best part of it was the more she got to know Lily, the more attracted she was to her.

Sitting together on the couch drinking a beer and sharing a plate of cheese and grapes, Frankie was enchanted by Lily as she talked about the town she called home. At first Frankie didn't think she was going to let down her Lily Lancaster persona and talk about anything real, but once she started it was like the floodgates had opened and they chatted away like long-lost friends.

"My whole family lives in Bell Buckle, Tennessee. We're a close-knit bunch. My parents host every holiday at their house. My sister's family comes and sometimes the neighbors too. It's super cozy and there's more food than we could possibly ever eat. My sister's seven-year-old twins run around like cute little maniacs. They rule the roost, that's for sure." Lily twisted a short lock of her blond hair around a finger as she talked. "Lord, I miss those kiddos most of all when I'm on the road."

Frankie twisted in her seat and tentatively placed a gentle hand on Lily's shoulder. Was it too soon for the familiar touch? They'd only known each other for a couple of hours, even if it felt like they had been connected forever. "They must be pretty special. You're lucky to have extended family close by. My parents live in southern California. I don't get back there as much as I'd like to, and even when I lived with them it was just the three of us. A big, full-house family gathering sounds great. My parents usually travel for the holidays and I end up staying here in Vegas with whichever of my friends are around." Truth was she couldn't remember the last time she was home longer than a quick overnight. Her last trip to Cali was right after Christmas and had stretched into a full weekend. That was probably it. Almost a full year had passed since. She really needed to schedule another visit with her parents. She missed them, but they were just so hard to pin down.

"Life in Bell Buckle is a little slice of heaven. I wish you could see it. Oh, gosh." Lily sniffed and laughed as she swiped at the tears that had suddenly appeared on her lashes. "I guess I'm a little homesick."

"Poor thing." Frankie leaned over the arm of the couch to grab some tissues from the box on the side table. "I didn't mean to upset you."

"You didn't." Lily smiled through the tears, shook her head, and blotted her eyes. She placed her hand on Frankie's knee and gave it a squeeze. "Actually, sitting here and swapping stories with you is the most at-home I've ever felt while traveling for work. You have a real gift for making people feel comfortable, did you know that?"

The compliment made Frankie's cheeks burn and the touch on her knee sent a jolt of excitement straight to her core. When Lily tipped her head onto her shoulder it just about did her in. The berry scent of Lily's shampoo set off another rustling in Frankie's chest and she hoped her budding nipples weren't obvious through her thin T-shirt. Just in case, she pulled one of the decorative pillows from the couch onto her lap to hide behind. "I feel comfortable with you too. And I liked hearing about your family back home, but maybe we should change the subject to be on the safe side."

Lily's body against her vibrated with laughter and Frankie casually draped an arm around her shoulders. "What topic would you like to broach next?"

Frankie ran her fingertips down Lily's arm with a featherlight touch. She liked the way Lily felt in her arms and she really wanted her to stay that way a little longer. She sucked in a deep breath and made up her mind right there. She was going to go for it. She placed her free palm on Lily's cheek to lift her head up and look her in the eye. It wasn't hard to recognize the same lust Frankie was feeling reflected in Lily's gaze. "I was thinking maybe something like this."

She pulled Lily to her and pressed her lips firmly to hers so there would be no mistaking how she felt. Their bodies fit together just right against the couch cushions, and Frankie's heart beat so hard she was certain Lily could feel it too. When they finally broke off for air, Lily's dreamy gaze met hers and she sighed contentedly, melting into her embrace.

"That was nice."

"It was so nice, I think we should do it again. Do you?"

Lily's sexy moan of agreement was all the encouragement Frankie needed to lean in for a second kiss full of promise for where the night would lead.

CHAPTER FOUR

Frankie yawned and stretched her long limbs. A little muscle stiffness after a night like she'd shared with Lily was to be expected. There had been minimal sleep since they'd climbed into bed, but that was fine by Frankie. A smile crossed her lips as she recalled how comfortably their bodies had melded together and how every touch had seemed perfectly natural as if they had been destined to collide. Her body hummed with the memory.

She reached for the aluminum water bottle on her bedside table. Rehydration was probably in order after the marathon of orgasms she had enjoyed before Lily got out of bed to take a shower. Lily had proven herself to be quite a star in areas other than country music. A tingle traveled through Frankie, making her nipples go hard again as her body remembered the sensation of Lily's soft skin sliding against her own. It had been a long time since someone had made Frankie come that hard. She toyed with the idea of joining the sexy blonde in the shower and having one last go before they went their separate ways for the day. Lily had mentioned a meeting with her manager despite the fact that she didn't seem to be in a big rush to get anywhere, but Frankie needed to make an appearance at the animal shelter before too long. Eventually she would be missed at work.

Frankie gulped her water and wiggled her toes along to the tune Lily was singing in the bathroom. She really did have an amazing voice. There would be plenty of time for the two of them to get together again. Lily was in Vegas for the next two weeks. Maybe Frankie would ask her out for dinner and take her to the steakhouse at the Rothmoor since that was where the country star was staying. She knew they had vegetarian options, so her preferences were covered. Then maybe later in the week Frankie could cook dinner for her. She had come across a new pad thai recipe she'd been keen to try out.

Before she had the chance to ponder date opportunities any further, Lily's phone rang on the bedside table. Normally Frankie wouldn't pay someone else's phone any attention, but she couldn't help but notice the name that showed on the screen identifying the caller: BOYFRIEND.

"Boyfriend?" she said aloud. Despite all the water she'd drunk, Frankie's mouth went dry. Why would a contact be listed in Lily's phone under the name *boyfriend*? "She was plenty into girls last night." Making jokes to the empty room was not making her feel any better. She blew out a sigh, sat her water bottle back on the table, and sank down under the covers. It didn't make any sense. The women had talked about a million things the night before and she never got the sense that Lily was hiding anything from her. Not even once. She swallowed hard against the rising lump in her throat. She really liked Lily, and there was no denying the crazy chemistry they shared. But she was not interested in being someone's vacation sidepiece. As the water shut off in the shower, Frankie's mind was made up. One night was all she could share with country music star Lily Lancaster.

Less than two hours after leaving Frankie's apartment— which included a quick detour to her hotel room for a fresh outfit to avoid any uncomfortable questions—Lily sat in the black leather desk chair in Angela's suite half listening to the list of rodeo events she was expected to attend with Brayden Judah over the next two weeks. She might have dodged the rundown the night before, but she was getting it full force to make up for it.

"I don't know where the hell you got off to last night, but Brayden said you didn't show for the poker night he hosted in his suite." Angela tapped a pen against the black portfolio in which she kept Lily's life organized. She sat with her legs crossed and one high-heel shoe dangling from her toes. It flopped and bounced against her heel in time with her words. "If you have a good reason for deviating from your scheduled appointments in the future, I hope you will alert us ahead of time instead of leaving us to wonder if our country superstar is dead in a back alley somewhere." Flop, flop, flop.

"I texted Bray. He knew I wasn't dead in a back alley somewhere." Lily twisted in her swivel chair. Why did Angela have to make everything sound so dramatic? The choice between being the odd girl out at Brayden's cowboy poker night or spending time with Frankie had been a total no-brainer. She had no regrets. Angela's schedule be damned.

Initially when Frankie rescued her from that inebriated handsy fan and whisked her off to Game of Flats, Lily had decided that she was a gal worth knowing. But then when Frankie had asked all those questions wanting to know about her life—her real life and not just Lily Lancaster music stuff—she was completely won over. Of course there was also the way Frankie loved the animals at the shelter and worked so hard to find homes for them. This was one interesting, big-hearted woman, and Lily was determined to get to know her better.

The thrill that came with spending the night with her was just icing on the cake. Lily's head went bubbly at the thought of the two of them naked together tangled up in Frankie's tie-dyed sheets. There was something special between them, and she couldn't just walk away from it because her manager would disapprove. As long as they kept things low-key and she didn't flaunt her sexuality in public, no one had to know who she was spending her time with anyway. It was time to stand up for what she wanted and demand she get it for a change. She only had to put her foot down. She was well aware what Angela's reaction would be when she 'fessed up to her feelings, but she was too damn excited to keep her thoughts to herself.

"I met someone."

The pen slipped from Angela's hand, clattering against the edge of the coffee table as it dropped to the floor. *"You met someone?"*

"The most awesome woman." Lily pushed off with her feet and sent the chair spinning in a full rotation. Her arms waved in the air like she was on a wild carnival ride.

"Oh God, Lily. What did you do?"

"You don't have to be such a dang buzzkill." Lily stuck her bottom lip out to ensure Angela would sense the magnitude of her stubborn vibe. She would not let her steal her joy. "I didn't do anything *unseemly*. I just met a great girl and spent a heavenly night with her." It sounded giddy even to her own ears—the lack of sleep was catching up with her. "She's not going to sell me out. She didn't even know who I was before we met, and likes me for me, not because I'm Lily Lancaster. I like her and I want to see where this goes."

Angela straightened her posture, sitting up to her full height and laser focused her gaze on Lily. Heels returned to shoes and feet returned to the floor. "Lily Lancaster, how many times do we have to have this conversation? You cannot date a woman. Absolutely not. Your brand is All-American Girl Next Door that every guy wants to fuck and every woman wants to be. It is absolutely key to project that image if you want to sell records. You *do* want to sell records, don't you?"

"Of course I want to sell—"

Angela didn't let her finish. "Then you can't be seen canoodling with women. Especially not here in Las Vegas. The whole reason you're in town is to be seen out and about with Brayden Judah, create a little buzz about you two as a couple, and enjoy a little boost in popularity."

"And to play a concert at the Amphitheater to close out Rodeo Week."

Angela flicked her long hair over her shoulder as if dismissing Lily's rebuttal. "A concert that was booked as part of the deal."

The concert had been part of the negotiations, but the only reason Lily had agreed to take part in the publicity stunt of dating Brayden Judah was because her dear friend had asked her personally—begged her, really—to do it. For the past two years he had been hearing the same heteronormative marketing speech from Angela as Lily. They both found the situation frustrating, if not infuriating, but agreed it was a small price to pay to further their careers.

"Give me a break. We both know Bray isn't any more interested in being coupled up with me than I am with him." Lily shook her head.

"I know that and you know that." Angela stood to make it clear the meeting was over and the subject was no longer open for discussion. "Let's just make sure the public doesn't know that."

As Lily entered the elevator to return to her own room, she pushed Angela's warning from her mind. She was a grown-ass woman who could handle keeping a personal relationship personal. If she had to keep her joy about the time she spent with Frankie hidden from her manager as well as the rest of the public, so be it. To seal her defiant decision, she tapped out a text on her phone to Frankie asking when they could get together again. She hit send and closed her eyes remembering the sensation of Frankie's lips exploring her body the night before. A tingle worked its way down her spine causing her pussy to clench.

Lily could be seen at rodeo events with Brayden Judah, and she could be discreet with her personal life, but there was no way in hell she could give up what she'd started with Frankie Malone.

CHAPTER FIVE

"Frankie, did you sign off on those reports I set on your desk after lunch?" Cara poked her head in the doorway of Frankie's office. "I want to get them into the files while I'm thinking of it."

"Oh sure." Frankie shuffled through the monstrous pile of papers that had collected over the course of the workday. Her eyes burned from staring at the computer screen. It had been a long afternoon. Her body had been present for her shift, but her mind not so much. Thoughts of her night with Lily alternating with the sighting of the boyfriend call had kept her brain preoccupied. "Here they are. I meant to return them to you. I guess I just got…distracted."

Distracted was one word for it. Frankie had spent a good part of the day resisting the urge to respond to Lily's texts. Ghosting someone didn't come naturally to her, but then again, neither did pursuing someone who was already in a relationship. The situation was hopeless. As the hours dragged on the worst part was Frankie couldn't shake her persistent deep sadness. She liked Lily. They had connected in a way Frankie hadn't with anyone else in a long time. And it wasn't just the scorching hot sex. Lily was funny and sweet, and even though she was apparently famous, she was remarkably genuine. She had even grown teary talking about her family because she was homesick and missing them. She didn't seem at all like the type to cheat on her boyfriend.

Cara's eyebrows furrowed and her normally cheerful expression darkened. "Are you okay? You don't quite seem like yourself today."

Frankie forced the corners of her mouth upward into a smile for her coworker. No need to spill her heart in the workplace. Boundaries. "I didn't get much sleep last night. That's all." It wasn't a lie. She hadn't exactly minded missing the sleep since instead the night was filled with what Lily had referred to as *mattress dancing*, but regardless, she was exhausted. "I'll catch up tonight and be back to normal for work tomorrow. Promise."

"It's not this place or the work I'm worried about. It's you." Cara placed a gentle hand on Frankie's shoulder. "You work hard all the time. Sometimes even on the weekend. If you're having an off day and need to knock off early, do it."

"I'm going to meet some friends in a bit, but I'll just be over at the café, so if anyone needs me…"

Cara rolled her eyes before making her exit. She clearly wasn't taking any excuses. "Go relax and spend time with your friends. I'll cover for you."

Thirty minutes later, sitting at their usual table in Café Gato with Mara, Jenna and Penny, Frankie's spirits had not lifted. The drama with Lily had taken her mind off Maeve and Zig's retirement plans, but while sitting in the café the topic was at the forefront of the circle's discussion again.

"I wonder what this place will be like under new management," Jenna pondered aloud and screwed her freckled face up before popping a bite of everything bagel into her mouth. Chewing didn't stop her from continuing, "Do you think the new owners will still let you have free rein here, Frankie? Do you think they'll still promote the shelter?"

"It wouldn't be much of a Café Gato without the *gatos*, even if they are just here in video form these days," Mara mused as she tipped her chair back casually onto its back legs. "It would just be Café."

"Put your chair down before you get hurt." Penny slapped at her friend's thigh as she scolded her. Her management mode didn't always shut off when she left her job at the casino. She twisted her long, blond hair into a bun and refastened it with hair sticks. An engineering marvel. "I guess they could just change the name. Do a total rebranding. It doesn't have to stay the Café Gato."

"Maybe they can move on to another animal," Mara suggested. "Café Perro or Café Pajaro?"

The others laughed, but Frankie pressed her hands over her ears. She didn't want the name of the café to change and she didn't want new owners to take it over. Café Gato was where Frankie and Mara first met, and that was how their whole friend group began. She wanted the comfort the coffee shop provided their group to continue. Forever. "Stop it, you guys. This isn't funny. This is the last thing I need today. It's been a…" To her surprise tears welled in her eyes. "A crap day."

Mara faked a gasp and put a shocked hand in front of her mouth. "Frankie, such language."

"Don't listen to her. You're obviously upset about something, and I'm sure it's more than Mara's poor Spanish." Penny dismissed Mara's teasing and turned in her chair to face Frankie, concern troubling her striking features. "Tell us what happened."

"Girl troubles?" Jenna asked pushing her bagel plate in Frankie's direction to offer her a comforting bite.

Nodding, Frankie waved off the carbs, a sure sign that she wasn't feeling herself. Even bread couldn't lift her mood. "You wouldn't believe me if I told you."

"Try us," Mara and Penny both said at the same time as they leaned forward to give her their full attention.

Frankie relayed the tale of meeting Lily while chasing Singe, fortuitously running into her again at the Rothmoor, and their incredible night together. Her friends all gasped, sighed and laughed at the appropriate parts and Frankie's heart ached when she got to the less-than-perfect ending to the story. She took a slow sip of lemonade to postpone the inevitable. Maybe she could skip that part.

"Wait a minute." Mara slapped her hand on the table, apparently needing to take control of the conversation. "You had sex with freaking country-music star *Lily Lancaster* and this story falls under the heading of *Girl Troubles*? It sounds like you should file this one under the heading Girl Super Good Luck."

Frankie gulped down her tangy drink, sighing as she set the glass on the table. "That's because you haven't heard the ending of the story yet."

"Oh, Frankie." Penny placed her soft, sympathetic hand on top of hers. She had a way of looking after the others in the group. It was probably part of what made her such a good manager. "What happened?"

"This morning she was in the shower and her phone rang. I didn't mean to be nosey, but I saw the name on the screen." Frankie swiped at the wetness on her lashes. She barely knew the woman. They had met less than twenty-four hours before and had nothing more than what amounted to a one-night stand. It was stupid that she was so upset that things didn't work out between the two of them. "It said 'boyfriend.'"

"Oh, yikes." Mara winced, clearly not expecting the story's turn.

"Yes. Lily Lancaster is with that rodeo dude, Brayden Whats-his-face," Jenna piped up matter-of-factly. "Everyone knows that, Frankie."

"*Everyone* knows that?" Mara squinted suspiciously at her friend. "Since when do you know the latest gossip in country music, Jenna?"

"I'm a Midwestern girl." Jenna grabbed the pointy peak of her fauxhawk in her fist and gave it a tug. Her tell for when she was talking bigger than the truth. "I'm a country-music fan from way back."

The other women joined Mara in narrowing their eyes at Jenna who was looking more sheepish by the second.

"Okay, okay." Jenna gave her hair one final yank then put her hands out in front of her, surrendering to her friends' questioning glares. "Lily Lancaster is really hot. She's on the cover of magazines and on TV. Who could miss her? Plus, you know Hayleigh is up on all that celebrity gossip. I guess I've picked up a thing or two along the way."

It made much more sense that Jenna's girlfriend would know who Lily was. Hayleigh would follow celebrities' lives with a great deal of interest. Frankie suspected that secretly she was hoping for her own breakout moment to arrive and thrust her into the A-List lifestyle, although currently Hayleigh's public appearances consisted of dancing on top of a bar *Coyote Ugly* style at a Vegas nightclub. Who knew what the future would hold? Anything could happen in Las Vegas.

"Can we focus on Frankie here?" Penny pulled the discussion back on track. "I guess you didn't know about the rodeo guy when you met Lily Lancaster."

"I didn't even know who Lily Lancaster was," Frankie admitted with a shrug. "All I knew was I met this sweet, fun, beautiful woman and had an awesome night with her, and then it was all over before it even really got started."

"Well, that's a little dramatic," Penny said as she straightened in her chair and drummed her pink, perfectly manicured short nails on the table. She was always the voice of good sense. "But I do know that both Lily Lancaster and Brayden Judah are staying at the Rothmoor—you didn't hear it from me. If it makes you feel any better, they are checked into separate rooms."

Lily was staying in a separate room from her boyfriend? That was weird.

As if on cue, Frankie's phone beeped with yet another text from Lily. The woman was relentless. She cleared her screen without bothering to look at the latest message. "She's texted a million times," she said with a sigh.

"Aren't you even gonna read it?" Jenna demanded. "At least give her a chance to explain. Let me see." She grabbed the device from Frankie and helped herself to a scroll through the earlier ignored messages.

"Lily doesn't even know that I know about the boyfriend," Frankie confessed. "I didn't tell her what I saw."

"Aw, these texts are adorable." Jenna's gruff expression melted into a much softer one she normally reserved for Hayleigh. "I think she really likes you."

"She is *so* adorable," Frankie said and a warmth rushed her body before she could remind herself she didn't want to feel that way about Lily Lancaster anymore. She recalled the whispered pillow talk exchanged earlier that morning before they made love for the last time. Sleepy but sexy utterances of good morning that had led to kisses, and teasing touches, and then so much more. She swallowed hard and steadied her resolve. That was then, this was now. "None of that matters anymore. I'm sure she's perfectly adorable to her boyfriend too."

"I get it." Mara nodded sagely and tipped her chair back again despite Penny's previous warning. "You don't want to be some celebrity vacation sidepiece."

"It's not even that. I just—" Frankie shook her head. There it was again—the sting of tears threatening at the back of her eyes. She glanced around the table at her friends. The group had always been honest with each other. There was no need to hold back on them now, no matter how stupid she felt saying it. "There was something different with Lily. She made me feel something *real* but I don't want to be a girl-crush fling to her. If that's all she wants with me then she can forget it. It hurts enough now—I don't need to put myself through worse."

"It doesn't look like that's all Lily wants from you based on these messages." Penny had taken the phone from Jenna and was taking a turn scrolling through Lily's unanswered texts.

"How can it not be? She has a boyfriend." Frankie pressed her lips tight together, holding in her frustration. She had been honest with her friends, but she had nothing else to say on the subject.

"Why don't you all come to Game of Flats tonight and drink it off. A good old-fashioned girls' night." Jenna's sympathetic gaze from across the table bordered on pity.

Frankie shook her head again. "No thanks. I think I'll go home, snuggle up in my jammies and have a *Gilmore Girls* marathon." She didn't miss the worried looks the others cast around the table at the suggestion of a couch-surfing, TV-fest.

"Are you sure?" Penny asked as she gathered the trash from their table. "Because Lauren and I are having a late dinner together, but it's nothing set in stone. We could totally hang out."

"And I'm working tonight, so I'll be at Flats whether you show or not. If you change your mind, stop in." Jenna's grin was equal parts encouraging and awkward. Comforting was not usually her thing, but she was really stepping up.

"I have a show. But if you need some late-night company, I'm your gal," Mara offered.

Frankie's heart swelled with love and gratitude for her friend circle. They weren't perfect, but they were always there for each another. She forced a smile and inhaled deeply. She would be fine. She would forget Lily Lancaster, and her achy breaky heart would return to normal.

Her phone beeped with another text and Frankie blew out an exasperated breath.

Eventually.

CHAPTER SIX

Saturday, Lily dragged her tired, sweaty self into her suite at the Rothmoor Towers Casino Hotel, tossed her cowboy hat onto the sofa, and plopped down beside it. Only after she'd propped her feet up on the coffee table in front of her did she realize her mistake in not drawing the balcony curtains first. The noonday sun was streaming into the room bright as hell. She should know—she had spent the past three hours out in it sitting by Brayden's side as he served as one of the judges at the Peewee Rodeo Competition. The kids were cute as could be and, giving credit where it was due, tougher than a two-dollar steak, but sitting in the front row of the dusty arena while the merciless Vegas sun beat down on her wasn't exactly Lily's idea of a good time. Damn. Brayden Judah really owed her for this one.

On top of that, she was still hurt that her numerous texts and calls to Frankie had gone unanswered. She didn't understand. It had been over twenty-four hours since she left Frankie's apartment and she hadn't heard a dang word from her. They'd had a great night together, that was for sure, and when they'd parted in the morning they'd shared a kiss that held the promise of more sexcapades to come. At least that was what she'd taken away. Lily grabbed her hat from the couch and fanned herself. Heat crept up her neck at the recollection of Frankie's full lips pressed against hers. She couldn't have possibly misread that. So what was with the silent treatment Frankie was serving up now?

Lily had been looking forward to spending more time with Frankie and getting to know her better, not to mention if she didn't get a hold of her and make some plans soon she'd be left with nothing to do but follow Brayden around to every hee-haw happening in town.

That sealed it. Lily Lancaster wasn't the type of girl to sit around and watch the world go by. If Frankie wasn't going to respond by phone, then maybe Lily could just happen to bump into her face-to-face and remind her of the good thing they had found the other times their paths had crossed.

Showing up unannounced at Frankie's front door seemed a little too forward, but a quick Google search on her phone gave her the name and address of that café Frankie had mentioned, Café Gato. After a quick shower and change of clothes, which included her trusty floppy hat and gigantic sunglasses disguise, she was out the door and on a mission.

One step into the café and Lily could see why Frankie was so fond of the place. The atmosphere was upbeat with friendly staff zipping around to keep patrons happy, and the cheerful brightly colored plates and mugs gave a pleasant caffeine buzz. Then she spotted the video of the shelter animals. She watched for a moment until footage of a familiar cat popped up on the screen. Stretched out in the sunny bay window seat of the animal shelter was…

"Singe!" she murmured as if a cat in a video could hear her much less respond. "Do you know where Frankie is, big boy?"

"Are you asking a cat in a video about Frankie Malone?" A woman's gravelly voice startled Lily. "Because you probably won't get much out of him. He's a cat of few words even in person."

Lily peered over the plastic rims of her sunglasses at the woman approaching her. "You know Frankie?"

"Do *you* know Frankie?" she countered as she came to a stop, shoving her hands into the pockets of her khaki cargo shorts and rocking on her heels. She squinted at Lily for a moment before her jaw dropped. "Oh my God, you're Lily Lancaster."

Lily pushed her glasses back up against her face and tugged the brim of her hat down lower. "No, no. I'm just someone who came into this cute café for a cup of coffee. And because I love cats," she hastily added.

Cargo Shorts wasn't buying it. Her pierced eyebrow jerked up and a smirk crossed her lips. "It's a good thing you can sing, Ms. Lancaster, because your acting skills are definitely subpar. I'm Jenna. Frankie is one of my best friends, and she mentioned she met you the other day."

"Please, it's Lily." She wondered what else Frankie had mentioned to Jenna. Based on Jenna's knowing look it was more than just that she'd asked for an autograph. "I've been trying to get ahold of Frankie. Do you know where she is?"

"I do." Jenna pulled a chair from a nearby table to her and straddled it. Her Doc Martens clomped down on either side of it against the vinyl floor. She was either settling in for a chat or physically blocking Lily from finding Frankie. "The thing is, I'm not sure she wants you to get ahold of her. She knows about your boyfriend."

"My boyfriend?" Her heart sank as she realized what had happened. Frankie had fallen for the Brayden Judah press stunt and now wanted nothing to do with her. She knew it was going to bite her in the ass eventually. At least Angela would be thrilled that her plan was working. Lily, on the other hand, was not. She shook her head, trying to rid it of the rising panic and come up with a good way to fix things. "No, there's been a misunderstanding. I need to explain it to her."

"Explain that you're dating Brayden Judah? Why don't you explain it to me and I'll pass it along the next time I see her?"

Lily blew out a long breath. She could appreciate the way Jenna was looking out for Frankie. She was only trying to protect her friend. Ironically, it was the kind of thing she and Brayden would do for one another. But letting Frankie in on her secret was risky enough. She wasn't ready to go around blabbing it to anyone. She shook her head sadly. "I can't. This is something I need to say to Frankie in person."

"I don't know if she wants to hear from you in person. From what she said earlier, she doesn't want to hear from you at all." Jenna tugged at the dark, spikey point of her fauxhawk as if she was struggling to make up her mind. "Frankie's not the kind of woman to chase after someone else's sweetheart, and she's nobody's sidepiece. She didn't know about Brayden Judah—hell, she didn't even know who *you* were before the two of you… uh…met."

The way Jenna's cheeks went red when she said "met" was evidence enough that Frankie had shared at least some of the details of their night together. So that cat was out of the bag. But now Lily had even more reason to talk things through with Frankie. She had to apologize for hurting her. That was the last thing she meant to do.

Lily swallowed hard against the lump rising in her throat before speaking again. "I would never treat Frankie like a sidepiece. I…I really like her. And I clearly owe her an apology for causing her to feel that way."

Jenna's expression softened. Her shoulders dropped and the hint of a smile even flickered across her face. A touch of tenderness under her tough exterior. "Okay. I'll tell you where she is. But if I hear that you hurt her again, well…just don't." She stood and replaced her chair at the table where it belonged. "She's over at the animal shelter next door. She had to work today."

Lily reached out to shake her hand. She recognized the gift she'd been given. "Thank you, Jenna. I appreciate it, and I promise I'll do better by Frankie."

Jenna gave her a nod. "One more thing before you go over there."

She stopped in her tracks ready to take another threat of bodily harm should she do Frankie wrong again. It was okay. A second chance with Frankie was worth it.

"Can I get an autograph?"

"I'm sorry, but Ms. Malone gave specific instructions that she was not to be disturbed. Not even if her friends came over from the café." The woman who greeted Lily at the front counter of the animal shelter had a giant smile, but her arms were crossed in a very no-nonsense stance.

Lily peeked over the top of her glasses to get a look at the woman's name badge. "Cara, I think maybe you misunderstood." She needed an excuse to get in and see Frankie and she needed it fast. She let out a light laugh and turned up the country twang in her voice. A little extra dose of Southern charm couldn't hurt. It always worked for Brayden. "I'm here to talk to Ms. Malone about a donation. I mean, I want to make a donation."

"You want to make a donation?" Cara frowned doubtfully.

"A sizable donation." She nodded enthusiastically, but Cara's wrinkled brow indicated she wasn't buying it. *Desperate times called for desperate measures.* She pulled off her shades, unleashing what she hoped was her full celebrity power. "I'm Lily Lancaster and I'm in town for a concert at the end of Rodeo Week, and while I'm here I'd like to make a donation to the local animal shelter. It's a thing I do, you know, I want to give back." She was rambling, but it was making sense in her mind. It was a small price to pay to get the chance to see Frankie and make things right. Plus Lily loved animals, so it was money well parted with. A win-win.

On his cushion in the window, Singe stretched and released a large yawn as if he was also unimpressed and suspicious of her motives for turning up at the shelter. *Et tu, Singe?*

Cara slid her hands to her hips as if she was running out of patience with the exchange even as Lily removed her floppy hat to reveal her identity further. "I'm supposed to believe that you are Lily Lancaster?"

"Yes." Lily stomped her cowboy boot against the floor. If full diva mode was what it took, so be it. "Why would I make that up?" Cara wasn't the only one whose patience was running thin. The longer it took for her to speak to Frankie and explain the situation, the longer Frankie would be spending thinking that what happened between them was just throwaway one-off and that Lily didn't care about her at all.

A second animal shelter employee had appeared behind the counter and gave Lily the hairy eyeball right along with Cara. "She *could* be Lily Lancaster. She has the same hairstyle." She shrugged noncommittally.

"That's because I *am* Lily Lancaster. Like I said, I'm in town for a show. Do you want to see my driver's license?" She dug in her tote for it.

"Sing," Cara said simply.

"What?" Lily stopped frantically riffling through her bag and looked from one woman to the other.

"If you're really Lily Lancaster, then sing a Lily Lancaster song."

Sing? That was all she had to do to prove her identity and gain access to Frankie's office? It was almost too easy. She opened her mouth to ask if they had a request, but a quick survey of their still-stern expressions made her think better of it. Best to just get down to business. She took a deep breath and belted out her latest chart-topper.

By the time she hit the chorus, the women were clapping along with big, happy smiles on their faces.

My momma told me that boy was just no good
He wouldn't treat me like a gentleman should
And I'd leave him, yeah, if I only could
My momma was right—

Her impromptu concert was cut short as a door to her left slammed and a third person entered the room.

"What is going on out here? You all are making a bigger racket than the dogs barking, and that's saying something." Frankie's face was pinched with anger until she spotted Lily. Then she went pale. "What are you doing here?"

"I, uh…you weren't returning my calls and I needed to talk to you about the other night."

The women behind the counter had found ways to look busy in pretense of paying no attention to the unfolding drama.

The big donation ruse was clearly exposed as just that. Frankie grabbed Lily's arm and dragged her back through the doorway from which she had just appeared.

Frankie pulled Lily into her office and slammed the door behind them before collapsing into her desk chair. Here was the country singer she was trying to ignore, giving the staff a private concert, and now that she had her in her office she had no idea what to do with her next. Part of her wanted to stand her ground and tell Lily to stay the heck out of her life, that she knew about her boyfriend and that was a deal-breaker. But another more traitorous part of her wanted to throw Lily down on her desk and pick up where they'd left off the other morning: kissing and touching and…

She shook that image out of her head. She couldn't let fantasy get the best of her. Lily would get the chance to explain her appearance at the animal shelter, then Frankie would politely send her on her way. Before that could happen Frankie had to yoga breathe her way back down to *polite*. "Have you lost your mind? What even was that out there? This is my place of employment not a karaoke bar."

"I'm sorry. The women behind the desk didn't believe it was really me, and they insisted I sing to prove it. I took off my hat and glasses, but they didn't seem convinced, and I guess that just goes to show my manager was right, I do need to get my face in front of the public more often."

The enchanting cherry-blossom scent of Lily's perfume swirled around the office and Frankie blinked hard twice hoping to clear her dizzy head. Lily's ramblings didn't explain the situation at all. Why exactly did she have to prove her identity to the front desk? And why did she have to look so darn pretty explaining it? Groaning, she buried her face in her hands. "I do not want to like you, but you make me smile so hard and you're just…so…irresistible." The words tumbled out of her mouth before she could stop them. She tried to course correct. "And infuriating."

"What do you mean you don't want to like me?"

"I can't like you, Lily." Frankie dropped her hands to her sides in frustration and met Lily's gaze. Despite that truth she wouldn't apologize for her stance on the situation. "You're with Brayden and I don't want to mess around with a woman who's already in a relationship. We're not going to happen." Her cheeks went hot. "Well, not again anyway. It's the way it has to be."

"Don't say that. It's not the way it has to be." Lily protested and then stopped short as if reining in her thoughts. She squeezed her eyes shut and shook her head as if choosing her words carefully. "Frankie, I'm not in a relationship with Brayden Judah. I mean, we're friends. We've been friends since we were kids, but that's all we are."

The words hit Frankie like a smack in the chest. All the air seemed to escape her lungs. Lily *wasn't* with Brayden? Had her friends' gossip-rag intel been wrong? It wasn't adding up. She must have misheard. "You're not with Brayden?"

She shook her head vehemently. "No. It's all a big…act." A hint of redness crept up her neck into her cheeks as she confessed, "Brayden and I have the same manager and she invented the narrative that we were a couple to hide the fact that we're both gay. You know, to try to keep us both mainstream popular. It sucks and it's backward as fuck, but it was just a temporary thing while were getting our careers established. Once Rodeo Week is over the charade will be too. But honestly, I'm not with Brayden."

The tension pinching Frankie's shoulders eased up for the first time in over twenty-four hours. She hadn't slept with someone else's girl. Lily being in a fake relationship with Brayden wasn't the best scenario, but it was a hell of a lot better than the alternative. It was temporary, and more importantly, it meant Lily's heart didn't belong to someone else. "So you're available." It was more of a question than a statement, but she tried to play it cool.

Lily sauntered around the metal desk between them and took both Frankie's hands in hers. "I am. Although I'm interested in someone."

Frankie's heart leapt into her throat and she started to pull away until the meaning of Lily's words hit her. "Oh! You mean me."

The laugh that passed Lily's lips was like music in the air between them as she pulled Frankie out of her chair so they stood face-to-face. "I mean you," she said before pressing their lips together in a tender kiss that made her feelings clear.

Frankie slid her hands down Lily's slim frame until they came to rest on her hips. She worked her thumbs into the belt loops of her jeans as her tongue teased Lily's bottom lip. Heat pulled between Frankie's legs and she briefly revisited that fantasy of throwing Lily down on her desk and having her way with her, but it was cut short when the dogs in the kennels started barking.

The women giggled at the interruption as they finally broke off the kiss. Lily placed a soft palm against Frankie's cheek. "That's the ruckus you compared my singing to earlier?"

"I didn't call your singing a ruckus, per se." The warmth of embarrassment filled her chest. "It was just, you know, loud."

"I'm kidding." Lily flashed that million-dollar smile that made audiences swoon. "But if you're feeling like you need to make it up to me, you could take me out to dinner tonight."

"I would like that very much." A romantic dinner, then maybe back to her place for a little...private time. It sounded like heaven, and the perfect way to spend a Friday night except— "Oh no."

"Oh no?"

Frankie blew out a breath. "I'd like to have dinner with you tonight, only there's something I have to do first." Frankie's brain reeled to come up with a way to make everything work. She had a commitment she had to keep, but Lily was only in town for a short while and she wanted to spend as much time as possible with her. Plus the way Lily's face fell when she said "Oh no" was downright heartbreaking. There was only one solution. "That is, there's something *we* have to do. Are you able to get your hands on some formal wear?"

When Frankie had asked her to rustle up something formal, Lily had no problem procuring a Vera Wang gown with a plunging neckline that was just as striking as its bold red hue. What she hadn't been prepared for was the pure enthusiasm of the young people at the Las Vegas LGBTQ Youth Center formal dance they were chaperoning. For starters, the crowd of teenagers was much larger than she imagined would show up for a Winter Formal held in such modest circumstances. The dance floor was jammed with kids dancing, singing along to the deejay's mix, and generally living it up. On top of that, the committee of youngsters and volunteers that had put the event together had worked the theme to the max and transferred the rec room at the center into a true Winter Wonderland complete with fluffy white snowmen and sparkling silver snowflakes hanging from the ceiling.

And perhaps the biggest surprise of the night was how much Lily was enjoying the time with Frankie and getting a little more of a peek into her world. "This is incredible," Lily said as she handed her date a cup of punch. "Does the center do this every year?"

"We actually do it twice a year. The Winter Formal around this time of year, and a prom in the spring." Frankie nodded as she accepted her drink. "Jenna's the one who deserves the kudos. She helps the kids on the committee make the theme come alive, building sets and whatever else is needed to decorate it all."

"The kids are the ones who think up the big ideas. I'm basically the muscle." Jenna shoved her hands in her tux pants pockets and gave a humble shrug. Her fauxhawk was neatly styled with the sides freshly shaved. Jenna's softer side had made an appearance in the presence of her girlfriend, Hayleigh, and she was much friendlier to Lily after Frankie swore the two of them to secrecy and clarified the Brayden Judah situation. "The dance committee is already talking about prom themes. I'm personally pulling for Game of Thrones. Can you imagine how cool it would be to build a dragon for it?"

"Dragons are cool, babe, but Game of Thrones is so five years ago." Hayleigh winced. "Maybe keep thinking on that one."

"I can't believe you do it twice a year." Lily shook her head. "That's so great for the kids."

"A lot of them don't feel safe going to their school dances or they're not permitted to bring the date they want to bring, so it's really important to give them an event that lets them be themselves. Plus, it's just so much damn fun." Hayleigh was a dancer who, in addition to her gigs in various Vegas shows and clubs, taught dance classes and yoga at the youth center. That explained the long, toned legs exposed by the thigh-to-floor slit in her slinky silver dress. She definitely had the appearance of the Ice Princess of their Winter Wonderland. "And don't let Frankie sell herself short on her part in this. She's vital to the center's programming. That's why they mentioned us in her Thirty Under Thirty article."

"Thirty Under Thirty article?" Lily's gaze zipped from one woman to the next. She was clearly missing something. "What's that?"

"Frankie didn't tell you she was featured in the annual Las Vegas Thirty Under Thirty list? Typical Frankie." Jenna grinned proudly at her friend. "The article just came out a couple days ago. It's a pretty big deal."

"It sounds like a big deal," Lily agreed, slipping her hand into Frankie's, proud to be her date for the evening for yet another reason. "Why didn't you say something?"

"Because I didn't want to make a *big deal* about it." Frankie's unamused glare locked on Jenna. "But it is a big honor and I am thrilled to be the recipient and that concludes the discussion on that topic for the night." She took advantage of their linked hands and gave Lily's arm a gentle tug. "I think this would be a good time for us to excuse ourselves and hit the dance floor."

As if on cue the music shifted from upbeat to a slow jam. They left Jenna and Hayleigh behind and wove through the crowd of partiers. Frankie was gorgeous in the vintage gown purchased at a thrift shop and upcycled by adding personal touches like hand-embroidered flowers along the scoop neck and ruffles in a contrasting fabric at the hem line. A few little changes to give it her own style. Frankie had said she had a few pieces in her closet that she'd redesigned over the years. Lily was lucky if she could sew a missing button back on a shirt and found this revealing fact about her date to be most impressive. She was learning quite a bit about Frankie Malone at their chaperone gig.

Just as they had found a good spot on the dance floor, a young girl who looked about fifteen stepped between them. *Here we go.* She'd catch hell when Angela found out she was at the LGBTQ center, but that was a risk she decided to take when she'd accepted Frankie's invitation. Lily was all set to sign an autograph or snap a selfie, but it was her date's attention the girl was interested in.

"Frankie, I need your help. Can we *please* talk for just a minute?" the girl whined. She nervously bit at her thumbnail while she waited for a response. The night was about the kids, not Lily getting the chance to dance with Frankie, so she nodded her encouragement in response to her date's questioning look.

"Sure thing, Grace. But is it okay if my friend Lily comes with us too? I promise she's very good with the advice too."

Grace turned to Lily, eyes wide. "Lily? You're that country singer Lily Lancaster, aren't you? Jackson said he thought you were, but we all thought he was full of crap."

Lily couldn't help but smile at the recognition, even if it did sort of feel like a backhanded compliment. When she had mentioned at the beginning of the night that she was worried about being recognized and distracting from the event, Frankie had assured her the kids would be way too caught up in their own world to pay the adults much mind at all. To her relief, it seemed Frankie had been right. She stuck out a hand to shake. "It's nice to meet you, Grace. I am, in fact, Lily Lancaster. Jackson was not full of crap."

"This time." Grace rolled her eyes and Frankie ushered them both off the dance floor to a quieter corner of the room.

"Now what's going on that is so important that we had to have a head-to-head in the middle of the Winter Formal?"

Grace nibbled at that same thumbnail again before diving in. "I really like Katie and I want to ask her to dance with me, but I don't know if she likes me that way." She took a deep breath before continuing, "How can you tell if someone likes you in a more-than-friends way?"

Frankie glanced at Lily before responding, and Lily gave her a noncommittal grimace to indicate she should take the lead on this one. Hell, Lily's major objective for the past few years was to pretend she was into someone. She was in way over her head advising anyone on actual relationship manners and mores. Fortunately, Frankie appeared to be a pro when it came to talking to young people about matters of the heart. "Grace, you can't tell by looking at someone if they might like you the way you want them to. But what you can do is put yourself out there and ask Katie if she would like to dance with you, or get a cup of punch with you, and get to know her a little better. Believe me, if she's interested she'll give you a sign."

Grace seemed to consider the advice, then looked to Lily for confirmation. "Really?"

Lily nodded enthusiastically. "I wholeheartedly cosign what Frankie said."

The teen sucked in a deep, fortifying breath and apparently made up her mind. "Okay, I'm going in." Without a backward glance she marched over to someone Lily presumed was the highly regarded Katie.

Lily found herself holding her breath while the two exchanged words, and when they both burst into grins and moved onto the dance floor she let out a sigh of relief. "She did it! You were amazing with her."

"Well." Frankie smirked and shrugged. "I might not have been so confident in my advice if I hadn't witnessed Katie watching Grace's every move this afternoon while we were decorating the hall. It was like she couldn't take her eyes off her."

"You knew she liked her."

"I had my suspicions." Frankie beamed and grabbed Lily's hand. She gave it a quick kiss. "I believe I owe you a dance."

After waiting for the last kids to get picked up by their rides after the formal was over, the women returned to the

Rothmoor Towers Casino for an elegant dinner at Daisy Jane's, the steakhouse. The meal included a decadent chocolate desert to which Frankie had only agreed because Lily had ordered one plate, two forks. In the end she couldn't decide if it was the sugar rush or the intimacy of sharing the rich dish that had her insides humming joyously. The evening had passed with easy conversation and so much laughter that when they left the restaurant Frankie wasn't quite ready to call it a night.

"What do you want to do now?" She raised her eyebrows enthusiastically, hoping to elicit an invitation back to Lily's suite.

"Mmm." Lily considered the question as linked her arm through Frankie's. "I don't want to say good night yet, that's for sure."

"Me neither." Frankie's chest felt full. They were on the same page at least. The women continued to meander through the gallery of shops that lined the walkway from the steakhouse to the main lobby. "We could check out the action in the casino."

"I don't know." Lily bit her lip as if thinking through the suggestion. "There's a great chance we'll run into Angela there and I'm having too much fun to deal with one of her buzzkill lectures about—" Before she could finish, she stumbled, nearly pulling Frankie down with her.

Luckily, Frankie was able to slip an arm around Lily's waist and steady them both before they hit the ground. "Whoa. Are you okay?"

"Oh my gosh, I'm so embarrassed." Lily's face flushed red and she looked around as if expecting people to be pointing and laughing at her misstep. But a woman staggering through the halls of a casino was not earth-shattering news in Las Vegas. "My heel broke." She reached down and plucked the errant piece of shoe from the rug.

With confirmation that Lily was okay, and a glimpse of the ridiculous bit of shoe, a snort of laughter escaped her. That caused Lily to guffaw as well, and then there they were, clutching each other and shaking with laughter until tears ran down their faces. All while dressed in formal wear, leaning against the wall in the hallway of a casino.

"I knew I should have worn my cowboy boots tonight instead of these stupid things." Lily gasped for breath and held up the remainder of her high heel.

Frankie swiped at the tears on her lashes with her free hand. "Why didn't you?" She was as much a fan of fashion as anybody, but she loved practicality just as passionately.

"I was trying to look fancy and impress you!"

"I took you to a teen dance!"

They dissolved into giggles all over again.

Finally Frankie slapped her thigh to summon sobriety and pulled Lily up from the wall. "I guess this puts a cramp in our plans to continue to paint the town, huh?"

Lily took a tentative, one-shoed step and nodded her head. "I think so. Let's hobble up to my room so I can get some sensible shoes. We can readjust the plan from there."

With Frankie's arm still around Lily's waist for support, the women crossed the main lobby of the casino. As they reached the bank of elevators, a male voice called out, "Lily Lancaster!" Lily turned and waved at the fan as Frankie dragged her into the elevator car.

"If you want to meet and greet with fans we can come back down when you have two matching shoes and we wipe those mascara streaks off your face." Frankie poked frantically at the door close button before the excited fan could catch up with them. She'd heard enough about Lily's manager to know this scenario wouldn't earn high marks with her. "We won't give Angela an excuse to give you a lecture on poise, grace and public appearances."

Once back in the privacy of Lily's hotel suite, Frankie sank into the plush white sofa while Lily fixed them wine spritzers at the bar. *A hotel room with a bar—damn, celebrities had it good.* Frankie had changed out of her dress into a Lily Lancaster concert T-shirt and a pair of Lily's boxer shorts. The soft cotton rubbed between her thighs as she crossed and uncrossed her legs. Her cheeks went hot as fleeting thoughts of these same shorts touching the intimate parts of Lily danced in her head.

"You should keep that shirt to start you down the path to loving country music." Lily's teasing voice over her shoulder snapped Frankie out of her impure thoughts. "I'm gonna turn you into a fan yet."

If the way her belly fluttered with excitement when Lily, who'd also changed out of her formal wear, sat next to her and their legs brushed together was any indication, Frankie was well on her way to being a fan. A damn hardcore fan. At least of Lily Lancaster.

Lily handed her a glass then lay back on the couch propping her legs on Frankie's lap. "Is this okay?"

Frankie took a sip of her drink to keep her mouth busy. The soda bubbles tickled her tongue. It had soared right past okay into fantastic. Since the moment she had lain eyes on her in that sexy red dress she'd been fantasizing about the ways Lily could touch her. Legs on the lap was nothing compared to what she wanted to do with this woman. But one step at a time. They had the whole night ahead of them. "This is perfect." She ran a hand gently along Lily's left ankle. "Does this hurt from earlier? Do you need ice?"

The blond strands of hair that had fallen from Lily's up-do danced around her face as she shook her head. "I think I'm okay without it, but I wouldn't say no to a leg rub."

Frankie squeezed Lily's calf muscles in her palms, surprised by the definition in her legs. Probably the result of hours of dance rehearsal preparing for her concert. Rubbing Lily's legs was a good start. She could work her way up from there.

She was happy the two of them finally had some privacy. No kiddos to chaperone, no friends getting up in their business, and most importantly, no fans trying to get a piece of Lily Lancaster. Frankie had her all to herself. Saving Lily from the camera phones snapping at her outside the elevator had given Frankie a rush. For that quick moment it was like she was Lily's protector, and that filled her chest with pride.

Lily's eyes fluttered closed and she moaned at Frankie's kneading. "Oh, you're good."

"You ain't seen nothing yet." Frankie kept her voice low, not wanting to spoil the relaxed vibe they had going.

"By the way, thank you for getting me out of that scene downstairs." Lily's eyes remained closed, but a serene smile graced her face. It was as if she could read Frankie's mind and knew she was replaying that memory of pulling her into the elevator.

"It was my pleasure." Frankie boldly moved her hands up above Lily's knees, applying pressure to her quads. "Is this okay?"

"Yes." Lily moaned again. "Your hands are magical. You can touch me anywhere you want."

Frankie's heartbeat kicked up a notch. She swallowed hard and fixed her gaze on Lily's glossy lips. *Don't get ahead of yourself.* "Anywhere I want?"

Lily's eyes flew open and she placed a gentle palm on Frankie's cheek, forcing their eyes to meet as she confirmed, "Anywhere."

A jolt of electricity shot through Frankie and she leaned in to kiss Lily's waiting lips. This was what she'd been dreaming of all evening, the chance to show Lily how much she had been craving her since that first night they'd spent together. When she thought Lily was involved with Brayden, she'd fought hard to keep those feelings down and shut them off. But now that she knew the truth, those urges were begging to be recognized. To be satisfied.

Lily broke off the kiss long enough to yank off her T-shirt. When they changed out of their dresses she hadn't bothered to put on a bra. Frankie gasped at the sheer beauty of Lily's creamy skin. A light sprinkling of freckles ran across her shoulders and the top of her chest. Her breasts weren't large, but they were perky, and the perfect weight cupped in Frankie's palms. She couldn't resist dipping down and peppering her cleavage with kisses.

Lily slipped her hands under Frankie's shirt, working the fabric up and finally pulling it off her. Her fingertips toyed with the lace of Frankie's bra. Frankie's nipples budded with anticipation as Lily's gaze ran the length of her.

"You sure know how to wear black lace." Lily's tongue darted out to moisten her lips. She pulled Frankie's shorts down to reveal her matching thong. "My God, you are beautiful."

Heat pooled between Frankie's legs as she stood and tugged Lily up from the sofa and into her arms. They kissed more urgently this time. Frankie probed her tongue into Lily's mouth. When Lily responded by sucking it, Frankie's pussy started to throb. While Lily shimmied out of her boy shorts, Frankie wiggled out of her lacy string.

Lily kissed her way down Frankie's neck, working her hands deftly at the clasp of her bra and removing it with one swift flick. For one moment they stood naked, face-to-face, eyeing one another hungrily.

"I've been thinking about this moment since I left your bed the other morning," Lily confessed. Her voice had dipped down to the sexy register Frankie recalled from the last time they were naked together.

"Me too." Overwhelming need surged through Frankie. She spun Lily toward the sofa and pressed against her back. She nipped greedily at her neck right below Lily's hairline and reached down to find her clit. She fingered her heat until she found the spot that made Lily's breath hitch. She drew slow circles with a light pressure while grinding against Lily's ass. When she picked up speed, Lily began to rock against her.

"Put your fingers in me, baby," Lily hissed.

As Frankie eased into Lily, her own excitement built. She continued rubbing against Lily's hip, sucking air to keep from tipping into oblivion. She traced her fingertips down Lily's back, bringing them to rest on the dimples at the base of her spine. Lily's back was the perfect mix of strength and grace. Her muscles flexed as they moved together. This was the contact Frankie had been craving. She wanted to take Lily to the point of no return. She wanted to witness her face as she climaxed. She sank her teeth into Lily's shoulder and growled, "I want you to come for me."

When Lily began bucking against her, she knew they were both getting closer to the edge of pleasure.

Lily tumbled onto the sofa and pulled Frankie down on top of her. She wrapped her legs around Frankie's waist and bit out, "Don't stop."

Frankie ground her pussy to Lily's, both of them slick as their juices mingled. Lily's fingers tangled in Frankie's hair, pulling her closer. Their mouths crashed together and Frankie finally gave in to pleasure. The wave that had been building crested. She arched her back and cried out.

Lily's legs tightened around Frankie's waist. Her eyes rolled and her lips parted in a silent scream as she came too.

They both gasped for air as Frankie eased down onto the couch and wrapped her arms around Lily. Her heart pounded and joy overrode her brain.

Lily was breathing just as hard and her face glistened with a sheen of sweat. Glowing. Her satisfied smile made Frankie's chest full. Holding Lily in her arms felt right.

She kissed the top of Lily's head and the scent of her flowery perfume filled her senses. Lily sighed contentedly and nestled into the crook of her arm. It was comfortable lying together that way, as if they'd done it a hundred times before. Frankie wasn't certain, but she suspected it was the sort of feeling about which country music ballads were written. Whatever it was, she knew one thing: she was a big fan of Lily Lancaster.

CHAPTER SEVEN

Lily plopped on the couch and tucked her feet under her, totally content to watch Frankie pour two glasses of orange juice at the bar in her suite. The women had spent a leisurely morning in bed and only rolled out of it minutes earlier when Frankie decided she had a citrus craving.

Lily had pulled up the playlist she had made for the two of them. True to her original statement, Frankie was indeed completely unfamiliar with country music, but Lily was easing her into it with country-pop crossovers. An upbeat Kelly Clarkson tune was pumping through the wireless speakers as Frankie shook her round, defined ass and poured juice. That girl sure made a thong and a threadbare T-shirt look damn good.

Suddenly Frankie spun around and summoned her with a wave of her fingers. Lily shifted in her spot on the couch mesmerized as Frankie shook her hips and sauntered over to her. A jolt of excitement shimmied down her body causing her pussy to buzz. Frankie took both of her hands and pulled her to her feet.

Following Frankie's lead, she moved in time to the music and shook her shoulders seductively. The women sang along as they held hands and danced. The more Lily moved, the more her body shook off the just-woke-up feeling and came alive. Frankie's eyes sparkled as she pulled Lily into her arms and spun her around before reeling her back in so close their hips bumped together.

They were having such a good time that they didn't hear the pounding on the door. Angela's infuriated voice finally got their attention, stopping them midgrind and sending Lily running to open up before her manager woke half the hotel floor.

"Lily, let me in."

"Okay, okay. I'm trying." Lily's nervous fingers fumbled with the security lock. Her blissful time with Frankie was swiftly drawing to a close, and as an uncomfortable sweat rose on her skin, her heart sank. This was not going to be pretty. As the bolt finally released, she jumped back out of the way of Angela's angry entrance.

"What the hell is going on in here?" Angela's gaze flashed between Frankie in her thong and tee, and Lily in her boy shorts and camisole as she marched through the room. "I tell you to cool it with the gayness and you respond by having some kind of lesbian-lover pajama party? Are you out of your freaking mind?"

Frankie tugged the hem of her T-shirt down modestly to cover her panties as she edged out of the room. "I'm gonna go get dressed."

"Good idea," Angela said without moving her laser-point gaze from Lily.

Lily clicked off the music and bit the inside of her cheek to stop herself from lashing out at Angela. Sure, her manager was treating her like a child, but losing her temper and acting like one wasn't going to help the situation. "We were just having a little fun in the privacy of my own hotel suite. No harm, no foul."

"No harm, no foul?" Angela spat back at her, incredulous. Her thickly lashed eyes were wide with outrage. Obviously she was not used to clients disobeying her. "Is that what you would call this?" She held out her tablet which was lit up with a picture from an online gossip magazine. Lily and Frankie strolling along the Las Vegas Strip on their way to the Rothmoor after the Winter Wonderland dance and looking more than friendly. The headline read, "Country Music's Newest Sweetheart Hits The Town With Mystery Gal Pal." "This is you hanging on that woman in public. As in *not* in the privacy of your own suite." She flicked at the screen with her fingertip to show another image of the pair, this time Frankie was pulling a grinning, mascara-streaked Lily into the elevator. "And then there's this gem. What's going on with your face there? Seriously, Lily, are you *trying* to sabotage your career?"

Damn that guy with the phone. Frankie had been right to stop the impromptu meet-and-greet by the elevators. Lily crossed her arms in front of her and shook her head defiantly. It wasn't as if they had been making out in public or had engaged in any lewd behavior. They had just gone out for a fun night. That fun night was at an LGBTQ youth center, but Angela didn't seem to know that part of the story and there was no reason she needed to. "We weren't doing anything wrong. All that picture shows is two friends walking down the Vegas Strip. It's no big deal."

Angela closed her eyes and blew out a long, exasperated breath as if she was struggling to hold on to her last shred of patience. "Lily, sit down and listen to me. And I mean really listen. You cannot be an out lesbian and Country Music's Newest Sweetheart. It's one or the other. If you are out your career will tank faster than you can say U-Haul."

Lily backed herself up to the arm of the sofa and perched on it, too stubborn to follow Angela's orders and actually sit. In the other room the shower had clicked on and Lily found herself grateful that the conversation wasn't being overheard. Poor Frankie didn't deserve to be treated this way. Blood had begun to pound in Lily's ears the moment Angela had referred to Frankie as *that woman*. "Her name is Frankie."

"What?" Angela's normally wrinkle-free brow dipped into a V in the middle of her head as if the response did not compute.

"Her name is Frankie," Lily repeated, not backing down despite her manager's hands-on-hips no-nonsense stance. "Not *that woman*. You don't have to like her, and you don't have to like us being together, but you at least need to treat her with a modicum of respect. She's done nothing wrong. Neither of us has."

Angela's eyes went wide again, but then her expression softened. Clearly this was not the response she expected from her charge. When she spoke again her voice held a gentler tone, almost as if she was looking at Lily as a person for once instead of a commodity. "Lily, it's not that I won't like Frankie—I'm sure she's a lovely person. In all honesty I think the two of you are cute as hell together in those pics. But I'm not here to tell you that you look cute. I'm here to tell you what is good for your career, and this"—she held the tablet with the online story out in front of her to emphasize her point—"is not good for it. As it is we're fighting a prejudice against women in country-music radio. A queer woman has no chance at all. Why make it even harder than it has to be."

Lily blew out an exasperated breath. She knew there was an unspoken rule in country radio that kept stations from playing two songs back-to-back by female artists. Even if one of those songs was by a group that had a woman lead like Sugarland or Little Big Town. Stations stuck by their stance that men didn't want that much femininity pushed on them. "It sucks that women have to fight for their place at the table. It's not fair."

"It's not," Angela agreed, "but it's the game we signed up to play. Women like you are leading the charge to change things by refusing to give up their seat and go quietly away."

"So doesn't it make sense that I should fight for my place as a woman who happens to love women too?"

Angela placed a hand on her shoulder and gave her a condescending look. "Absolutely not. That's one woman too far. Like I said in the first place, you don't have to make it even harder on yourself to succeed. You've worked hard to get to where you are, we both have, and I'm trying to do what's best for your music career. Please let me."

Lily's gaze scanned the upmarket suite before landing on the glass doors to the balcony and the stunning view of the Las Vegas skyline. She was a damn long way from the open-mic nights she had played at dive bars back in Tennessee before Angela. Her manager had always steered her in the right direction. She had no reason to doubt her now. She needed to play nice and stay the course. "Okay. I'll be more careful from now on."

"Yes you will." Tender moment gone, Angela was totally back to business. She flipped the tablet back around and began poking at the screen with a stylus that seemed to magically appear in her hand. Lily held back a giggle. That thing was like an appendage that automatically extended from Angela's wrist as needed. "And you'll do some damage control too. Starting with a well-documented and photographed dinner with Brayden Monday night. We'll fight fire with fire."

Dinner with Brayden seemed reasonable enough. She had been attending the rodeo events with him as agreed, but she had been neglecting her BFF since their arrival in Las Vegas. She had been too busy with Frankie. It would be nice to have a little one-on-one time with him. She could share some good eats with her best bud, catch up on their personal lives, and smile pretty for some publicity shots. No problem. "Sounds good. Name the place and time—I'll be there."

"That's step one." Angela gave a slow, thoughtful nod before her eyes lit up with inspiration. It was a look that warned Lily to brace herself for what was coming next. "For step two you'll do a special song dedication to Brayden next week at the concert. A little shout out to your main man. It will be perfect timing with so many rodeo fans attending the show. The crowd will eat it up."

Dedicate a song to Brayden as if he were her lover? Lily inwardly cringed. Being seen out together and letting fans draw their own conclusions was one thing—dinners, events, pictures together for press—that all felt somewhat normal. But saying something like that in front of a full audience—that felt a lot more like lying. Not to mention like a crime against nature. Brayden was like a brother to her. Lily chewed her lip and considered her options under Angela's expectantly raised eyebrows. She shrugged noncommittally. "I don't know about that. It seems a little much."

"That's why they call it show business—it's all about the show." Angela shrugged then tucked the tablet under her arm as if the topic was no longer up for discussion. All traces of that humanity and girl power they'd shared earlier had gone with the wind. "You need something solid to counteract the curiosity floating around regarding your mysterious *gal pal*." She dragged the last words out making them seem especially ominous, but then she shook her head to dismiss the conversation. "Look, I'll write something up, you'll say it at the concert and the fans will be happy. No big deal."

As the door closed behind her departing manager, Lily caught a glimpse of her own reflection in the mirror above the wet bar. Her blond hair was disheveled from the impromptu dance party with Frankie. Their untouched glasses of juice sat abandoned. Her heart dipped low at the thought of making a dedication to Brayden that she would rather be saying to someone else.

Angela was right—Lily had worked hard and made sacrifices to get to where she was. She didn't want to give that up. But there was a nagging at the back of her mind that she just couldn't shake. Where did not telling the truth end and lying begin?

Frankie blinked her eyes repeatedly as they adjusted to the lighting in the café after being outside in the bright Vegas afternoon sun. Her morning had started off wonderfully when she woke up in Lily's arms, but ever since, the day had gone nowhere but downhill.

First there was the awkward arrival of Lily's manager while the couple was dancing around in their underwear, a show Frankie had meant for Lily's eyes only. After that, Lily's mood had shifted and Frankie had to rush off to the animal shelter before she had the chance to help her work through it. Then Frankie had suffered through hours of work planning for the scheduled meetings next week in which she would beg their corporate sponsors to loosen the purse strings a little more to assist with the never-ending needs of the animals at the shelter. It was just after two o'clock in the afternoon, but she shouldn't have had to work on a Saturday in the first place and she was worn out.

"Hey, *mystery gal pal*!" Mara greeted Frankie loudly from across the café.

Frankie grimaced as she joined Mara and Jenna at their usual table, hooking her messenger bag over the back of the chair before sitting down. She should have known the group would get a hold of the gossip-rag article. There was no way they would let that slide.

"Where have you been all day, *mystery gal pal*?" Jenna pulled a face as she chimed in on Mara's joke.

Frankie stuck her tongue out at her friends in response to their antics. They were like a dog with a bone and were not going to let it go until there was nothing left to chaw. "This gal pal's whereabouts today were anything but mysterious. I've spent the whole day in my office glued to my computer preparing for meetings with potential donors. This is in no way my favorite part of the job." She slouched down in her seat and propped her tired feet up on the empty chair beside her.

"It does sound a bit boring." Mara twirled a wooden coffee stirrer between her fingers like a mini baton. "Let's get back to the much more interesting *mystery-gal-pal* situation. I have screenshots if it helps jog your memory. This is a classic." She held out her mobile with the picture from the online article filling the screen.

"I, for one, think it's a lovely shot. You look beautiful and so happy. I love your dress." Victoria McHenry, Mara's girlfriend, arrived at the table just in time to rescue Frankie from the merciless teasing. Her red hair danced around her pretty face as she planted a light kiss on the top of Mara's head. She grabbed a chair from a neighboring table and pulled it up, joining in without missing a beat. "Rein it in, Mara. It's just a picture of two women enjoying each other's company and walking down the

Strip. It's not as if the paparazzi caught them doing something scandalous."

"That's exactly what Lily said to her manager, although that woman wasn't having it." Frankie waved a hand in the air dismissively. "She does not like me."

"What do you mean she doesn't like you?" Mara leaned forward in her chair, all traces of teasing gone. It was totally okay for Mara to harass her friends, but she was the first to raise her hackles at anyone outside the group committing such a heinous offense.

Frankie shrugged. The topic had tingled at the back of her head and pulled at her heart enough without making too big of a deal about it to her friends. She just wanted to forget the crap that morning and get back to the good part of hanging out with Lily, but her friends were staring at her waiting to hear it all. She had to come clean. "I overheard a discussion between Lily and her manager this morning. She doesn't think Lily being a lesbian is good for her country-music star image. That's why she does so much press with that rodeo guy Brayden Judah. They're trying to give their fans and the public in general the sense that they're a couple, but of course they're totally not." She realized she may have revealed more than Lily would want her to, but the group could be trusted. Still she hastily added, "And that information does not leave this circle. You're all sworn to secrecy now. Seriously."

Each woman around the table raised a hand in turn indicating their solemn vow.

"He's her beard!" Jenna grinned. "Isn't that sly?"

Frankie nodded. Jenna had simplified the whole thing a bit, but she wasn't that far off the mark. "Something like that. So when these photos showed up online this morning her manager went ballistic. Now she's making Lily be seen out in public with Brayden even more to try to counteract it all."

"What does Lily think of all this?" Victoria's eyes were full of concern as she put a comforting hand on Frankie's forearm. The excellent bedside manner that made her such a good nurse often came to the fore in how she treated her friends. She was also good at assessing a problem objectively, a skill she probably honed in the ER at Sunset General.

"She doesn't love the arrangement, but she does love her career. It's a small price to pay to get what she wants." Frankie shrugged. "It won't be forever, just until the end of Rodeo Week. Anyway, the whole reason she's here in Vegas is because of the publicity stunt, so ironically, if she wasn't pretending to date him I would have never met her."

"Huh." Jenna grunted. "She had me fooled. I thought she was in town for her concert."

"The concert is a happy benefit," Frankie replied simply.

"As long as you're happy." Mara's frown indicated that she did not share that emotion. "Something about the situation doesn't sit well with me. It's bad news to get involved with someone that deep in the closet. I don't want you to get hurt."

"You're sweet, but I'm fine." Frankie dismissed her friend's concern, grateful for the distraction of Maeve bustling over to their table with the coffee pot and extra mugs.

"Hi, girls." Maeve set an oversized mug in front of Frankie and an iced cappuccino by Victoria. "Extra whipped cream, just how you like it, Victoria. Refills for you two?" She held the pot up for Mara and Jenna.

"Fill me up. I've got a long night of entertaining the masses ahead." Mara pushed her cup toward the edge of the table and slumped comfortably back in her seat. "How go the retirement plans, Maeve?"

"There's so much to sort out you wouldn't believe," Maeve said as she leaned on the back of the chair on which Frankie's feet were propped. "If Zig and I weren't ready to retire before, we sure are now."

Frankie's coffee seemed to slosh around uncomfortably in her stomach. With everything else that had happened that day she had managed to push the unpleasant subject of Maeve and Zig's retirement from her mind, but here it was again dancing around in the sunshine. Real as anything.

Maybe there would be a complete overhaul and their hangout wouldn't even be a café anymore. The coffee shop could become a drycleaners, or a pawn shop, or anything really. There had to be some way to keep things from changing so drastically. She gave voice to the first idea that popped into her mind. "Maeve, have you and Zig considered keeping the café and just running it from afar? I'm sure you could find someone who could handle the day-to-day stuff—manage things for you."

"Oh no, honey." Maeve waved her dishrag like she was surrendering a battle. "We love you girls like our own and owning the café has given us a wonderful life here, but it's time. We're ready to let it go."

Before Frankie could come up with another idea to keep Café Gato in its owners' hands, Zig signaled with a wave for his wife to join him at the counter and Maeve was back to work.

"Ugh. They're really retiring." Frankie sighed and slouched in her chair. "I was hoping they had changed their minds."

"It's a bummer," Jenna agreed.

A *bummer* was putting it mildly. What would happen to the café? Where would the women hang out if the place wasn't the Café Gato anymore? Her deep thoughts were interrupted by Victoria's gasp as Mara grabbed her drink and stuck her face in it.

"Mara, what are you doing?" Victoria shrieked at her girlfriend.

Mara set the mug back down to reveal her mouth surrounded by the white foamy whipped cream from her iced coffee. A comedic effort to lighten the mood of the group. She gestured at Frankie. "Suit up, *mystery gal pal*, now you have a beard to go to the rodeo with too."

"You're buying me a new coffee," Victoria quipped and slapped at her arm.

Frankie laughed along with the others, but the joke reminded her of Mara's earlier comment. Deep in the closet was somewhere Frankie had never been, nor was it somewhere she intended to go. She knew where she stood on that, but whether Lily was going to be able to find her way out was a whole other issue.

CHAPTER EIGHT

Late Sunday afternoon, Frankie swiveled on her seat at the counter and nursed her cup of coffee. Lily was meeting her at Café Gato the minute she finished her Rodeo Week obligations for the day. Frankie was treating her to an afternoon of Las Vegas must-dos. First, the magic show at the Tropicana, then dinner at the MGM Grand Buffet. A perfect Vegas date.

The excitement about spending one-on-one time with Lily was making waiting especially difficult for Frankie, but a crowd was forming in the café in anticipation of the poetry slam they were hosting and the people-watching was superb. The crowd was young—hipsters mostly—but there was one elderly couple that caught Frankie's attention. The gentleman pulled his wife's chair out for her. She lined up two pink packets of sweetener next to his mug before pouring the cream for him. They were a couple so obviously in love, a warmth just seemed to radiate from them. They anticipated one another's needs and met them with a caring touch. Frankie's heart squeezed as they grasped hands on the tabletop. This was the kind of love she always dreamed of finding. Someone with whom you could be together yet be yourself, unafraid of who saw how unabashedly in love with one another you were. Shout-it-from-the-rooftops love. That couple had it, and that love was out there somewhere for Frankie too.

"No, Kitty. Not you too." Maeve's desperate voice cut into Frankie's thoughts. "Café Gato is still functioning. We have a full house for the poetry slam. Just because Zig and I are retiring doesn't mean…Kitty? Are you there?" Maeve groaned and slammed the receiver back into its cradle.

Frankie loved that the café still had a landline behind the counter, but she didn't love the look of panic etched across Maeve's face. "What's wrong? What was that about?"

"It's about the second person this week who quit with no notice, leaving me down not one, but two servers tonight. Word's getting out that Zig and I are selling and the mass exodus has begun." Trance-like, she patted at the perspiration on her brow with her counter-wiping rag. "How am I going to handle this lot and the counter too?"

Frankie surveyed the café. Patrons had continued to trickle in for the slam while she'd been waiting for Lily. *Waiting for their best-of-Vegas date.* She'd been looking forward to seeing Lily all day, but the panic on Maeve's face was tugging at her heart. Maeve and Zig had always been there for Frankie, and now they needed her help. *But those plans with Lily…*

"It's going to be a long night." Maeve sighed and tucked the towel back in her apron apparently resigned to her fate.

"No, it's not." Frankie slid off her stool ready to hop to action. "You've got me. I can help."

"I can't ask you to do that," Maeve argued. "You have your big date. You'll miss your show."

"You're not asking me. I'm offering." Frankie tied an apron around her waist. "Besides, we can catch that show another time. They do it twice a day at the Trop."

Frankie was already weaving through the café tables refilling coffee cups when Lily walked through the door a few minutes later. She'd sensed her presence more than noticed her come in and when she glanced up, there was Lily, flashing her million-dollar smile and wearing the floppy hat and sunglasses that probably weren't fooling anyone. She was the picture of beauty even in her disguise. A sharp pain pinched between Frankie's shoulder blades as she realized she had to break their date and let Lily down.

"What's with the apron? You ready to get going?" Lily took Frankie's free hand and wove their fingers together. The wattage of her smile dialed up a notch and Frankie's heart sank.

"Listen, Lily, I'm so sorry to do this, but something's come up and I have to cancel on you." Frankie's gaze flicked over to the counter, hoping more servers had miraculously appeared, but all she saw was Maeve rushing around trying to keep customers happy. She had to get back to helping out, no matter how badly she was aching to run out the door with Lily and get on with their night. "Two servers called out and if I don't help Maeve, she'll have to deal with all this herself. So, I'm sorry, but I can't leave right now."

Lily's face fell as the words registered and Frankie had to look away at the flash of disappointment in her eyes. She hated that she was ruining Lily's day. "No, it's okay. I understand." She pulled off her sunglasses and squinted at the full café tables. "You're gonna cover *all this* just you and Maeve?"

"Yeah." Frankie followed Lily's gaze and wasn't surprised to find more than one patron waving at her for a refill. "And I gotta get back to it." She turned to go, but Lily's hand on her arm pulled her back.

"Wait." Lily yanked off her floppy hat. "Where do I get an apron?"

Two hours and many poems later, the poetry-slam crowd had finally cleared out. Lily swiped the back of her hand across her sweaty brow and carried her bussing bin to the next dirty table. She was collecting the empty plates and mugs while Frankie swept the floor. This was the last way she'd expected her Sunday evening to go, but she was just happy she got to spend time with Frankie.

It had been a good long time since Lily flexed her food-service muscles. She and Brayden had worked together at a diner back in Bell Buckle the summer after junior year. She was a waitress and he bussed tables and washed dishes. It had only been for a few months, but the skills had come right back to her as she worked that evening at Café Gato. She got into a real groove and actually had fun. The poets were inspiring, the patrons friendly, and the double chocolate muffin Maeve had passed her on her break was absolutely divine. There was something special about the little café, and it was easy to see why Frankie loved it there.

Lily traded her dish bin in for a fresh rag and turned up the radio. As she wiped down the counter, she shook her hips along to the beat of the classic rock power ballad blasting out of the speakers.

"I love this song!" Frankie gushed as she sidled up to Lily. "Let's dance."

Frankie twirled her around the café while Lily belted out the lyrics. Even Maeve got in on the act, swaying behind the counter with her hands in the air.

Lily's whole body buzzed with joy. There was no feeling that compared to doing what she loved while wrapped in Frankie's arms. Who would have guessed that a canceled date could lead to this magical moment? A tingle tickled up her spine as she spun around and hit the final high note.

Zig came out from the kitchen to applaud the performance, and Maeve bustled over with a take-out menu and a sharpie.

"I can't believe it, a real rock star right here in our café!" She waved the menu. "You've got to sign this to prove you were here. I'll hang it up and show it off to everyone who comes in. It will probably increase the value of the café!"

Lily giggled, but signed her name while Frankie beamed at her. True to her word, Maeve went straight over to tack it on the bulletin board by the register.

"Well, it wasn't the date I promised you. We missed the magic show." Frankie grabbed Lily's hand. "But there's still time to hit the buffet at MGM."

"I think that sounds *grand*." Lily gave her a squeeze.

"MGM Grand. I see what you did there." Frankie rolled her eyes, but she laughed too. Lily liked that she made her laugh. "All this and funny too. I feel like the luckiest girl in the world."

Lily linked her arm through Frankie's, but she knew she was wrong. Only one girl could be the luckiest in the world and based on the way her heart wanted to burst with joy, she was pretty sure it was her.

CHAPTER NINE

Frankie locked her computer and pushed back her chair away from her desk. After a long day of meetings, her Monday was finally over. Enough was enough. She rolled her neck from side to side and tried to shake off the stress that had troubled her upper back for the better part of the afternoon. The sigh that escaped her lips couldn't be helped as she hitched her bag on her shoulder and headed out of her office. She wished she was on her way to see Lily, but instead she would be spending the evening alone. Lily's manager was insisting she do some stupid publicity stunt dinner with Brayden Judah to make up for their slip up with the paparazzi Friday night, so Frankie would be left to her own devices.

She called out goodbyes to her coworkers on her way through the lobby of the shelter, but as she stepped out into the cool evening air she changed course and popped in next door to Café Gato for a Danish as a treat after her solo heat 'n' serve microwave dinner.

The familiar and comforting buzz of activity in the café was a balm to Frankie's stressed-out soul. She sucked in a deep breath of the sweet-smelling air. It gave her the punch in the arm needed to shake off her bad mood. The tension in her neck eased up. Was it possible for air to be caffeinated?

"Frankie!" Maeve's happy smile split her face in two as she greeted her with a wave from behind the counter. "Cup of your usual?"

"Not today." Frankie shook her head as she settled in on one of the red vinyl swivel stools at the counter. "But I will take a double-chocolate Danish to go."

"You got it." Maeve hummed an upbeat tune as she reached under the counter for a carry-out box and fetched the pastry from the glass display case. She bundled the bakery box in twine before placing it in front of Frankie.

"You're certainly in a good mood."

Maeve pulled a dishrag from the pocket of her apron and wiped some crumbs from the vintage countertop. "Ever since Zig and I made up our minds about retiring it's like a weight has been lifted from my chest."

Ever since they'd made up their minds about retiring there'd been a weight put on Frankie's heart, but she kept that thought to herself. No use in stealing Maeve's joy. But still, that worried voice whispered in the back of her mind. What were her friends going to do without their usual hangout? Maeve and Zig had put so much of their life into the café. Maybe there was still hope. "So you're sure about this?"

"Oh yes, honey." Maeve positively beamed as she leaned her elbows on the counter, taking a break from her bustling around. "We did that computer phone call thing with the grandkids last night and told them their Nonni and Pop Pop would be coming to live near them soon and they got so excited. You know how little ones can get. They are real blessings, those kids."

Frankie opened her mouth to argue the finer points of being a café owner, but the far off, dreamy look in Maeve's eyes made her think better of it. It was selfish of her to put her social life ahead of Maeve's longing to be with her family. Both Maeve and

Zig had earned it. They deserved to enjoy their retirement. She mustered up a smile as she reached across the countertop and gave the older woman's hand a gentle pat. "I'm really happy for you two. Your grandchildren are some lucky kids to have you coming their way."

Grabbing her bakery box by the string, Frankie slid off her stool. With any luck Maeve would mistake her watery eyes at the thought of losing the café for tears of joy for the retiring couple. She said goodbye and made a beeline for the door before her emotions got the better of her.

Her great escape didn't get her too far though. She nearly plowed right into Jenna and Hayleigh on the sidewalk right outside the café.

"Woah!" Jenna wrapped her dog Rex's leash around her hand to keep him from straying too far as they made their sudden stop. "Where's the fire, Frankie?"

"Hey, you guys. Sorry." She bent down to give Rex, their German shepherd black lab mix, a rub on his head. As she straightened up again she fixed her features in what she hoped was a brave face. "I was just talking to Maeve about their retirement plans and I guess it got to me."

Hayleigh wasn't fooled. She slung an arm around Frankie's shoulders and pulled her into a half-hug. "You're upset about the questionable future of the café. I get it. I am too."

"We all are," Jenna chimed in as she smiled and nodded at the guy who had stopped and asked if it was okay to pet Rex. "It's probably harder on you since you help out Maeve and Zig so much. You are pretty much part of their staff."

Maybe that was part of the problem Frankie was having with the sale. "Café Gato is like my home away from home. I don't know what I'll do without it."

"If you want a new place to hang out, you could always start spending more time at Game of Flats." Jenna shrugged. "I'll even get you your own rag and let you wipe down the bar if it helps."

Frankie didn't mind hanging out at Flats, but spending the bulk of her free time at the dark, loud bar? No, thank you.

Game of Flats was nothing like the sweet, buzzy, sunny vibe of Café Gato, and most likely Jenna knew that, she was just trying to help. "I appreciate the offer. Let's call it a 'maybe' for now."

The friends shared a sad smile and her heavy mood returned. At least she still had her double-chocolate Danish to lift her spirits when she got home.

"Oh! What a pretty doggie." The cheerful voice of a little girl who was eyeing up Rex broke the gloom. She looked to be around eight and she bounced on her toes with excitement at making a furry friend. "Is he friendly?"

Hayleigh turned and addressed the girl. "He is and he loves meeting new people. You can pet him if you'd like. And if it's okay with your mom."

After checking for her mother's approving nod, the girl knelt in front of Rex and gave him an enthusiastic rub about the ears and neck. Rex was clearly a fan of her two-handed technique.

"Cammie, be soft," her mother reminded her before turning back to the group of women. "She's always asking when she can get a dog of her own, but I'm just not sure I'm up to the task. It's hard enough raising kids, I've got two more at home, without throwing a pet in the mix."

"You never know, a dog might help you keep the kiddos in line. Like how a sheepdog helps a farmer round up his flock," Hayleigh joked, but Frankie saw an opportunity in the mother's confession.

"The Clark County Animal Shelter is right on the corner there, one storefront down." She pointed down the block. "Even if you're not ready to adopt, they're always happy to have volunteers help walk the dogs. You and Cammie should check it out sometime. You can volunteer as much or as little as you like."

"Mmmhmm." The woman nodded as her gaze followed Frankie's down to the shelter then back to Café Gato. She peered into the big storefront window. "I've never noticed this café before. I could go for a hot drink." Emphasizing her point, she hugged herself and brushed her arms with her hands as if to warm them.

"They make a mean hot chocolate," Jenna confirmed, causing Cammie to hop back up on her feet and press her face against the window.

"Can we get some hot chocolate, Mommy?"

"That sounds good to me." The woman took her daughter's hand, said goodbye to the group, and led the way into the café.

Jenna grinned and patted Rex's hindquarters. "I hope you get some commission for that, bud."

"Seriously, Maeve and Zig should strongly consider greeter dogs to hang out on the sidewalk and draw people in." Frankie's pulse quickened as inspiration struck and an idea started to take form. "They could get dogs from the shelter to do it. That way it would be a win for all. The dogs would bring passersby into the café, but at the same time potential adopters would stop to meet them. Imagine if Cammie had met a dog that could potentially go home with her today. That could have been a total love connection!"

"I'm not so sure Cammie's mom would have been on board with that." Hayleigh frowned before quickly adding, "But greeter dogs sounds like a cute idea."

"Sure, but Maeve and Zig don't exactly need a cute idea to bring in business now," Jenna pointed out matter-of-factly, but when Hayleigh elbowed her in the ribs she softened her tone. "You could still suggest the idea to the new owners, if they don't tear it down or turn it into a vape shop or something."

"Just stop." Hayleigh narrowed her eyes at her girlfriend and grabbed her hand. She glanced apologetically at Frankie. "On that note, we should get going. We both have to work tonight."

"See you tomorrow," Frankie called as her friends took off down the sidewalk.

She tightened her grip on the bakery box strings and tried to drum up enthusiasm for the frozen dinner waiting for her at home. The excitement of a new idea to bring business to the café had surged though her like a lightning strike. In that moment she had been ready to jump into action and flesh out a plan to put in motion. She felt alive.

But now her heart sank as she gazed through the café window to where Cammie and her mother were enjoying hot chocolates. Jenna was right. Things were changing at the café, and Frankie was going to have to accept it. She could have all the big ideas her brain could churn out, and shove Danish in her face until she exploded in sugary glory, but one way or another Maeve and Zig were retiring and there was nothing she could do to stop it.

Lily took Brayden's offered arm and climbed out of the car. She lifted her chin and smiled as paparazzi documented the couple's arrival at the Emerald Isle Casino, home of Failte. A nice steak and potato dinner all dolled up with Brayden should set the fans straight.

Straight. How Angela wanted the two of them to be.

She shook the curled ends of her shaggy hair to knock those negative thoughts from her head and forced her smile even bigger. She would focus on how fun it was to be all dressed up and out on the town with her best friend. She owed Brayden that much.

Brayden had cleaned up nicely from his rodeo duds. Although he was still wearing jeans, they were a fashionable dark-wash denim and he had paired them with a soft, white button-down shirt and a very classy tan jacket. Ruggedly handsome. His outfit was the perfect complement to her body-hugging, sapphire blue dress. The spaghetti straps and thigh-baring short length gave Lily the heady sense that she was oozing sex appeal. She had texted Frankie a few selfies before she left her suite wishing she could have showed her the outfit in person.

Knowing that the photographers wouldn't be allowed to follow them in, Brayden gave the cameras one last wave as they entered the casino.

"I am so ready to get to the good-eats portion of the evening." He grinned at her as they crossed the main lobby to the escalator that would take them to their dining destination. "I will say, Las Vegas has been very good to my stomach." He patted his belly contentedly but seemed to reconsider his statement. "Although probably not quite as kind to my waistline."

"I bet you burn a million calories a day doing all your rodeo stuff." She gave his shoulder a friendly bump. Why did they even say things like that? It seemed like guys lost weight just by thinking thin thoughts. "I wouldn't worry about it all that much. Or at least not until after we enjoy this feast. I mean, we've earned this. Not to mention it's on Angela's dime."

As they entered the steakhouse they were met by the delicious aroma of expensive, grilled meats. Lily's stomach growled in anticipation. While Brayden spoke to the maître d', Lily took in the décor of the Failte. Very old-school boys' club with its mahogany-paneled walls and mounted deer and ram heads. One wall featured a built-in tank filled with silver fish that shimmered in the water like shiny silver coins.

Lily smiled at the frolicking fish. It reminded her of the tank at Frankie's house, although her fish were multicolored as opposed to this monotone bunch. Cheerful and vibrant like Frankie's personality. Only Frankie would name every single fish. She also knew the name of every animal at the shelter. Lily found that impressive and a testament to how much Frankie loved those animals even if she did seem more than a little over her job.

The night Lily had stayed at her apartment Frankie had confessed she wanted to buy a house with a yard one day so she could get a dog or two. Lily could understand that. She missed her family's golden retriever, Parker, but being on the road wasn't exactly ideal for having pets. Another sacrifice for her career, she realized with a sigh as Brayden signaled to her by twirling his pointer finger in the air that their table was ready.

Once they were seated and their drinks served, Brayden leaned back in his chair and studied Lily intently. She peeked back at him from behind her menu. "Is there something on my face? I mean, you would tell me if I had something on my face, right?"

Brayden cracked his knuckles and shuffled his feet under the table. "No. You look flawless, Lil. I'm just…" He paused to take a sip of his fancy, dark beer. He licked the foam off his top lip before he went on. "I'm trying to figure out why my very best friend in the whole world is blowing our cover for a little tail."

"Brayden!" Lily gasped and slapped her menu down on the table. "Frankie and I aren't like that—I care about her. And I don't appreciate you talking about her in those terms."

Instead of looking remorseful, Brayden crossed his arms across his chest like a roadblock and narrowed his eyes at her. Suddenly all traces of the *golly gee boyish charm* had dried up like the beer on his face. "I don't like people thinking the girlfriend of rodeo star Brayden Judah is running around on him. And I don't appreciate that you're going back on our deal."

Lily leaned in closer in an effort to keep the conversation private. If Brayden wanted to go down this road she was prepared to hang on for the ride. "A: we are not a real couple, and B: you sound ridiculous talking about yourself in the third person. Get over yourself." She sat back up poker straight in her chair as their salads were delivered and thanked the server gracefully before continuing, "I'm not going back on our deal. I've explained to Frankie what we're doing and she completely understands. I am truly sorry about getting caught by the paparazzi and that jerk with the cell phone, and like I told Angela, I'm going to be a *lot* more careful going forward. Promise."

"And?" Braden prompted.

Lily picked up her utensils, done with her speech—and the topic as a whole—and ready to enjoy the food in front of her. "And now I'm going to eat my salad."

"And you're going to do what Angela asked you to do and make that dedication to yours truly at the concert Friday, right?"

The fork in Lily's hand slid out of her grasp and clanked against the salad plate. Embarrassed heat rushed her cheeks as she hastily grabbed it again and sheepishly glanced at nearby tables to determine if her faux pas had disturbed any other diners. Brayden had caught her off guard with his insistence and was still staring at her expectantly. Clearly he had fallen in line with Angela's demands and was using the dinner as an excuse to strong-arm Lily into doing the same. A ball of fire burned in her belly. Brayden was supposed to be her best friend. He should be glad that she met someone that she cared about and that she was happy. Wasn't that what friends did? She felt the dull thud of anger pound behind her eyes and she struggled to keep her voice low and calm. "I haven't made up my mind about that yet."

"What's there to make up your mind about?" Brayden asked around his mouthful of salad. "We agreed to do this for the positive press. Both of us. The song dedication is part of the package you agreed to." He shook his head. "Come on, Lil. Since we've been here at Rodeo Week I've gotten a taste of the good life. I'm so damn close to crossing over here. People recognize me. Once I get the chance to prove myself in the arena this week I'm gonna totally be big time. I just need your help. Besides, you know I'm good for your image too."

"I know Angela *said* that." Lily poked her fork at a grape tomato, her appetite suddenly diminished. What she had expected to be a fun evening with her best friend was quickly becoming a first-class guilt session. "I feel weird about saying something like that in front of all those people. It feels dishonest. Not to mention, I really like Frankie and she'll probably be at the concert."

"But you said Frankie knows the truth about us." Brayden wiped his hand over his mouth, not bothering to use the napkin parked in his lap. He lowered his voice which only made his words sound like a hiss. "She knows we're not a couple. That this is all for show. Look, you don't want people figuring out that you're gay, do you? Do you really think your career can survive that?"

The comment stung as much as if Brayden had slapped Lily's face. He was supposed to be her best friend. He was supposed to be a source of support. They had their own personal gay-lesbian alliance. Instead he was regurgitating Angela's words and making it seem like Lily was ruining her life because she'd fallen for a girl. She opened her mouth to sputter a retort, but before she could form any actual words she felt tears tingling at the back of her eyes. Crying at dinner would definitely ruin the façade of her romantic night out with Brayden, but if she sat there any longer that was exactly what was going to happen. Pressing her lips together to hold in the impending sob, Lily pushed her chair back, stood up, and dashed out of the steakhouse as fast as her stilettos would take her. She didn't stop moving until she was alone in the back of a cab and heading back to her suite at the Rothmoor Towers Casino Hotel.

It was over an hour later when Lily's pajama-wearing, couch-sitting, brooding-over-her-hurt-feelings time was interrupted by a knock on the door. Based on several ignored phone calls, she had a pretty good idea of who it was.

"You left without your dinner." Brayden grinned sheepishly and held out a foil-wrapped package shaped like a swan. Las Vegas never failed to be too much, right down to the takeaway from a restaurant. When Lily didn't react he continued, "Can I please come in? I want to talk."

The ride home had given Lily the time she needed to calm down and consider things from Brayden's perspective. The rest of the time she had spent feeling bad that she was half-assing both her agreement with him and her budding relationship with Frankie. She didn't like it, but there didn't seem to be a way to be entirely one way or the other without sacrificing something. At least not until after Rodeo Week. The least she could do was hear what he had to say. She stepped aside and let him in.

He set the foil to-go package down on the bar and sat on the couch, patting the cushion next to him, inviting Lily to join him. He took her hand in his big, rough one and tipped his head to the side to regard her. He was a much sweeter Brayden than she had left at the steakhouse.

"I owe you an apology. I was a real ass back there," he began. Lily opened her mouth to respond, but he stopped her. "Let me get this out first before Yee-haw Too-Big-For-His-Britches Cowboy Brayden comes out again. I should have never said those things about you and Frankie and I'm sorry that I did. I'm sorry that I hurt you. You're my best friend and I'm happy that you've found someone like Frankie who you really like being with. In fact, I think I'm a little jealous."

"You're jealous that I met a girl?"

"Not exactly because you met a girl," he corrected. "I'm jealous that you met someone special and that you are brave enough to admit it." He rolled his eyes dramatically. "Please, have you not seen some of the hot buck cowboys around here? I'd love to rope me one for myself, but I can't. Because I can't trust that someone won't blab it to the world. And if they do that, I'm afraid I'll be tossed from the rodeo circuit like a drunk gal on a mechanical bull. It's too much for me to risk and basically I'm a big ol' chicken."

She finally smiled as she gave his hand a reassuring squeeze. "You're not a chicken. You love the rodeo and you've worked hard to get here." Her words sounded awfully familiar. "I'm afraid too," she confessed with a sigh. "Not that Frankie will out me. I trust her. But that *someone* will. I'm afraid that the fans will turn on me too like Angela keeps saying. And that will be the end of it, you know? My dreams will just slip right out of my hands. But there's something about this woman, Bray. The way I feel when I'm with her makes me want to test the boundaries of what I've been told. She makes me want to live on the edge and see what happens."

Brayden nodded and murmured sympathetically, "Mmm hmm."

Now that their friendship was back on familiar ground, Lily felt lighter. "I'm sorry I haven't been a great fake girlfriend lately. I promise to do better for the rest of Rodeo Week."

"Oh, honey." He slipped his hand out of her grasp and patted her knee. "You're always the best in my book. You make up your own mind about the concert thing. Whatever you decide is fine by me. But you're still coming tomorrow to Rodeo Row, right?"

"Absolutely."

"You should bring Frankie. I'd really like to meet this special woman of yours." He nodded encouragingly as if to hypnotize her into agreeing. "They have a ton of vendors lined up. They deep fry every kind of food you can think of, I swear. I'll even get her the beer garden wristband. They have a bunch of craft beer breweries handing out samples, and the wristband gets you all you can drink."

"Well that seals the deal." Lily laughed, relieved that their moods seemed to have improved drastically. It was good to be back on track with her dearest friend. They were lucky to have each other, just like Frankie was lucky to have her group. That thought gave Lily an idea. "Actually, could I bring a few friends to Rodeo Row too?"

That good old country boy charm flashed across Brayden's face and he spread his arms in a welcoming gesture. "The more the merrier!"

CHAPTER TEN

When Lily had invited Frankie and her friends to go along with her to an event called Rodeo Row, she'd had no idea what they were in for. Frankie didn't usually attend Rodeo Week since she had never really been into country music or cowboys. But since it was an excuse to spend time with Lily, Frankie had enthusiastically accepted the invitation. And because her friends were the awesome people they were—and generally good sports all around—they all agreed to the outing as well.

Rodeo Row was a big, cowboy-themed fair with vendors selling their wares, carnival-style games, and even a few rides. The group met after lunch and went straight to the beer garden since Brayden had come through with complimentary wristbands. Frankie, Lily, and Mara staked out a picnic table while Jenna and Hayleigh went for the first round of beers.

"Oh, I hope they bring one of those big bags of peanuts back with the drinks." Mara straddled the bench and plopped herself down. She picked at the edge of her flannel shirt where she had cut off the sleeves to give it a rugged cowboy flare. Her braided-leather wrap bracelet slid along her wrist with each pluck. "It's so great that you can just toss the nut shells right on the ground."

Lily laughed at the joke, but Frankie gave Mara a shove in the shoulder as she sat down beside her. "You promised you were going to be nice."

"I know. I'm sorry." Mara grinned and tipped her head to the side to show her remorse. "Lily, thank you for inviting me. I've never attended a Rodeo Week event in all my years living in Vegas and I appreciate you opening my eyes to it."

"You're welcome." Lily smiled sincerely. "I hope you have a good time."

"How could you not have a good time with all this beer here?" Jenna set refillable plastic mugs of beer on the table and sat down next to Lily. She had also dressed in the spirit of the day in a light denim shirt and a cowboy hat. "Bull riders really know how to party."

"And everybody is so friendly," Hayleigh gushed and slid a mug across the table to Mara. No doubt she had turned more than a few heads in her ridiculously short ripped-off daisy dukes and cowboy boots. With her plaid shirt tied at the waist and her hair braided in long blond pigtails she gave off an interesting country schoolgirl vibe. Frankie felt sorry for people who looked at Hayleigh and thought her packaging was the best part of her. Through the years of their friendship Hayleigh had proven time and time again that her inside was every bit as beautiful as her outside. From her volunteer work at the LGBTQ center, to the way she still wrote handwritten thank-you notes. She had a big love for her friends and her community.

"People are always friendly to you," Mara said between sips of foamy beer. She waggled her eyebrows suggestively. "You make friends everywhere we go. Why is that, Hay?"

"It's a gift," Hayleigh quipped with a shrug. She knew her worth.

"So what are we drinking?" Frankie sniffed at her beer. It was a little darker than her usual brew, and it had a definite hops scent. She wasn't completely off put by it, but she wasn't sold at first glance.

"This, my friends, is a Pokey Bull Horns IPA." Jenna nodded sagely. "Brewed specially for Rodeo Week."

"Isn't that name the cutest?" Hayleigh grinned. "*Pokey Bull Horns?* They had a cute little bull logo too."

"Speaking of bulls, is anyone feeling brave enough to give that mechanical bull a try?" Mara lifted her mug to indicate just beyond the edge of the beer garden where the Buckin' Bronco Challenge was set up. The placement seemed like it was selected deliberately to entice those who had swallowed a hearty helping of liquid courage.

All eyes turned to Lily as the only true country girl in the bunch, but she swallowed her mouthful of beer and waved them off with both hands. "Don't look at me! I'm just a musician. I've never rodeoed before either. I think Jenna should give it a try. At least she's got the hat for it."

Frankie reached across the table and grabbed Lily's hand. She liked how easily she had slid into her friend circle. To hang out in their group you had to be able to take it and dish it out in equal measure, and Lily had proven she could do just that. Frankie's chest went warm as Lily's ocean-blue eyes sparkled with laughter. Lily gave her a wink and slipped her hand out of her grasp to pick up her beer mug for another sip.

"You should give it a try, babe." Hayleigh slipped one arm around her girlfriend's waist and pulled her closer. The two were always touching each other. They'd been that way since the day Frankie met them at the animal shelter years before when they adopted Rex. Frankie wanted to hold on to Lily like that—easy and comfortable. Two parts of a pair.

"I'll do it, but not until a couple more of these." Jenna held her empty mug in the air. "Sisters, join me in another round and then let's get out there on Rodeo Row and see what the vendors have to offer. On the way in I spotted a booth with belt buckles for every occasion. I need to take a closer look at that. I think a belt buckle could be a real statement piece in my wardrobe."

The women all held their mugs up in solidarity and grinned at each other before rising from the table to refill their mugs. As the group passed the mechanical bull they gawked at the brave souls giving it a try.

"They should get one of those at Game of Flats." Mara waved in the direction of the bull. "That would really bring the crowds in."

"I'll talk to management and see what I can do." Jenna played along. "Something like that would look great in the back corner of the bar opposite the pool table, right?"

Mara snapped her fingers, upping the joke even farther. "Oh! See if they can get it put in before Birthmas!"

Lily spun around so fast she had to grab her cowboy hat to keep it from flying off her head. Her face clouded with confusion. "Birthmas?"

Frankie laughed at her reaction. These women had been together for years and had a lexicon all their own. There would definitely be a learning curve as she continued to hang out with them.

"Mara's birthday is three days after Christmas," Frankie explained. She was used to Mara's quirks but was aware they were an acquired taste. She had to ease Lily into them. "Every year she insists on throwing a big party because she thinks if she doesn't, her big day will get lost in the holiday shuffle."

"That's how we got *Birthmas*." Jenna rolled her eyes. "God forbid Mara's not the star of the show."

The other women laughed but it didn't seem to faze Mara one bit. She grabbed onto the wooden fence separating them from the bull-riding area and leaned back dramatically as she sang out, "Happy Birthmas to me!" She snapped back upright and waggled her fingers at Lily. "You have to come this year. It's the party of the season."

"You should totally come. You don't want to deny the Birthmas girl," Frankie agreed. The sparkle in Lily's eyes as she joked with the group made Frankie's heart flutter. "Plus, I'd kinda like it if you were there too."

"How can I resist an invite like that?" Lily giggled. "Tell you what, I'll see what I can do."

"I'm holding you to that." Mara pointed a denim-blue-tipped nail at Lily. "Enough of this bull." She tipped her head toward that bucking machine. "Let's get some beer."

Once everyone had a fresh drink, the group headed out into the main vendor area. The number of booths that lined both sides of the venue was amazing. People selling everything from deep-fried pickles to life-sized, hand-carved wooden bears. The size of the crowd was also surprising. Who knew so many people flocked to Las Vegas for Rodeo Week? Hayleigh grabbed Jenna's hand and excitedly pulled her along from one display to the next. The other three friends followed behind.

As they meandered along, Frankie glanced down at Lily's hand, wanting to grab it in her own, but she knew better than to try in public. It was too risky with so many people around. The price of being with Lily was respecting Angela's rules on this issue for the time being, and while Frankie didn't love it, she accepted it as better than not being with Lily at all. She settled for linking her arm through Lily's. She wasn't shocked when Lily linked on to Mara as well making the three of them into a "clearly just friends" chain.

When Jenna and Hayleigh stopped at the belt-buckle booth, Lily pulled the others to a neighboring table housing a display of beautiful hand-crafted silver and turquoise jewelry.

"Oh, look at this." Mara picked up a two-inch-wide cuff bracelet adorned with stones and slipped it on her wrist. She posed with her arms in an X in front of her. "I'm a wild-west Wonder Woman!"

The woman working the booth smiled politely, but Frankie's scalp prickled with embarrassment. "Be nice, Mara," she scolded yet again. "I'm sure a lot of hard work goes into a handmade piece like that." She intended to say more, but a necklace on the display table caught her eye and distracted her.

She picked up the delicate piece and let it drape over her fingers as she admired the craftsmanship. It was a single turquoise teardrop pendant, but the sterling silver setting was exquisitely detailed with a fine polka dot pattern. The silver chain glistened in Frankie's hand. "This is gorgeous."

"That one is two seventy-five," the woman behind the booth said helpfully. Frankie didn't miss that fact that she left off the qualifier as if that took away the pain of the price. Two seventy-five what? Rocks? Good deeds?

"If you like it, you should get it." Mara shrugged without looking up. She had managed to cover her entire forearm with silver bracelets and seemed to be mesmerized by the effect.

Frankie appreciated her friend's support, but her animal-shelter salary didn't exactly allow her to drop three hundred dollars on every pretty accessory that caught her eye. "I like it, but I don't know." She rubbed her thumb lightly across the smooth stone before returning the piece to the display. "I'll think about it and stop back on our way out later." She thanked the booth lady, grabbed Lily's arm, and directed her away to where Jenna and Hayleigh stood watching a man sitting in front of an easel drawing caricatures for eighteen dollars a pop.

"Hey, wait up you guys," Mara called as she scrabbled out of the bracelets stacked on her arm and rushed to catch up with them. "So, where to next?"

"I promised Brayden I'd go see him while he's signing autographs," Lily volunteered. "He's doing his celebrity cowboy thing. You girls want to come with me?"

"Meet a real live rodeo star?" Jenna nodded. "I'm in."

"Your interests are as varied as they are bizarre." Mara grinned at her friend. "Let's do it."

The vendor area of Rodeo Row had been busy enough with the shoppers, but the section roped off for the autograph signing was absolutely jam-packed. Frankie was stunned by the size of the crowd and she smiled at their enthusiasm for the sport. In front of every cowboy's table was a long line of excited fans—men, women, and children alike.

When they finally squeezed their way through the throng to Brayden's table, Lily stuck both hands in the air and waved for his attention. "Hey there, cowboy!" she called out to him and he immediately stood up as if he recognized the golden voice of the country crooner.

"There's my girl." He beamed and pointed when he spotted her. Lily ran to him, leaving the group to join him behind the table.

Frankie cringed as Brayden pulled Lily to him and kissed her right on the mouth. Not a quick kiss either. It was a long, drawn out, *has everyone had a chance to snap a picture of this?* kind of kiss. When he picked Lily up and twirled her around his fans hooted and cheered, but Frankie's jaw dropped with shock and a lump rose in her throat. It was one thing to know that Lily and Brayden were going around acting like a couple—it was a very different thing to have to witness it firsthand. And in front of her friends too. It sucked.

"Hey, you okay there?" Mara slung an arm around her shoulders.

"Oh, me?" Frankie waved a hand in front of her face, half to dismiss the thought, half to ward off the tears prickling at the back of her eyes. She fumbled with the plastic mug in her hands. "No, I'm fine. I'm just…I think I'm ready for another beer."

Mara's gaze darted knowingly from Lily and Brayden back to Frankie. She pressed her lips together as if assessing the situation, then nodded sagely. "Yeah, I think a beer sounds like a good idea. Let's head back to the beer garden."

"Oh! And the mechanical bull!" Hayleigh chimed in.

Frankie glanced over at Lily again. The lip lock with Brayden had ended, but now she was cornered by her manager and neither of them looked pleased. Maybe Lily needed a beer too. "Let me just rescue Lily from that." She nodded in the direction of the frowning women. "And we'll get the heck out of here."

Lily scrubbed a hand over her face and blew out a deep breath. She squinted in the Las Vegas afternoon sun at the tablet screen Angela had shoved in front of her and was now frantically poking at with her stylus. How was this same thing happening to her again?

"As you can see," Angela hissed as she stabbed at the pictures, "the story they picked up on was not 'Lily Lancaster and Brayden Judah Share Romantic Evening Together,' but rather, 'Lily Lancaster Runs Away Screaming From Man.'"

"They did not call it that." Lily frowned. Sure the stunt didn't go the way they had expected, and she might be to blame for that, but Angela didn't have to be so damned dramatic about it. The actual caption under the photo of her read, *Lily Lancaster's hasty getaway from dinner with cowboy boyfriend, Brayden Judah.* "And I didn't scream when I ran. I just cried a little."

Angela looked down her nose at Lily, obviously not amused. "They actually titled the article 'Dine And Dash' and as you can see, they had more than that one photo to back it up."

Lily winced as Angela scrolled through pic after pic of her all dolled up in her fancy cocktail dress hightailing it out of the main entrance of the Emerald Isle Casino and practically diving into the back of a taxi. At least nobody in the restaurant saw her cry, she thought as she mentally berated herself for the bad decision to leave Brayden that night. She would take her small victories where she found them.

Unfortunately Angela wasn't letting up. "Was there a reason you were incapable of sitting down at a table across from Brayden and having dinner with a smile on your face?" She plucked at the lapel of her stiff suit jacket as she spoke, probably hot from being overdressed at an outdoor venue. Even at a rodeo event Angela didn't seem able to dress down her all-business wardrobe. She was on point from her no-nonsense bun down to her sharp-toed stilettos. Maybe uncomfortable footwear was why she always seemed so grumpy.

There was no good answer that was also truthful, so Lily didn't bother making excuses. She couldn't change the past. "Now what?"

Angela sighed as if the answer was obvious. "Now you'll have to make further reparations. You'll start by sitting your ass down next to Brayden at that table and smiling pretty like half of a perfect couple. A little fawning over Brayden now and again wouldn't hurt either. A touch here and there. A loving glance. Prove to the public that you are here to stand by your man."

Lily's gaze darted from Brayden signing autographs and chatting with excited fans to Frankie and her friends who were staring back at her expectantly. It wasn't that she minded hanging out with Brayden for an afternoon, it was just that she had been having so much fun with the girls and she would rather be doing more of that for a change. Especially since the clock was ticking on her time left in Las Vegas. She'd promised Brayden she would do better by him, but she wanted to squeeze in as much with Frankie as humanly possible.

"It's not a suggestion." Angela interrupted her thoughts as if she could read them. "You need to do this."

Lily's shoulders sagged as she exhaled in surrender. "Let me just tell the girls so they're not standing there waiting for me all day."

Frankie was already approaching her as Lily left Angela's side. From the disappointment on her face she had already figured out what was coming. At least she would be spared the embarrassment of having the conversation in front of the whole group.

"It looks like I'm gonna have to stick around for a while. You ladies should go on without me." Lily could barely look Frankie in the eye. She was letting her down, there was no getting around it. "The paparazzi caught my great escape from dinner last night, so now I have some spin to do. I swear, I've never been so popular with those guys."

"What's that thing about any publicity being good publicity?" Frankie's tone was joking, but her smile didn't quite reach her eyes. She had taken the afternoon off work to go to Rodeo Row and now Lily wasn't able to hang out with her. Lily gave her credit for attempting the joke at all.

"Not according to Angela." Lily shook her head sadly. "You girls go on. I'll catch up with you later if I can."

Frankie grabbed her hand and gave it a half-hearted squeeze. "We'll be at the beer garden for a while. Text me if you can get away," she said simply before turning and rejoining the group.

Mara, Jenna, and Hayleigh all waved to Lily as they headed on their way out, but Frankie didn't look back.

CHAPTER ELEVEN

On Wednesday Lily spent the whole day following Brayden around, but for once it wasn't because anybody insisted she do it. It was because she needed a distraction while Frankie was at work.

By the time she had finished up at Rodeo Row and the press events that had followed, it had been too late to meet up again with Frankie. At least that was what Frankie said, citing an early start at work the next morning when she texted a little after nine. Lily felt terrible about being pulled away from the party and her friends, especially after Frankie had taken the day off work.

She very much wanted to make it up to her and that was why the next day saw her dashing up the stairs to Frankie's unit, flowers in hand, heart in her throat.

She glanced at her phone. Ten after five. The women hadn't been specific about a meeting time, they'd just left it at "after work." This seemed as good a time as any. She shoved her phone in her back pocket and knocked on the door. Sounds of movement inside the apartment indicated someone was in there, but there was no response. She waited a few beats, shifting the flowers to her other hand before she knocked again. "Frankie, it's me."

Clumsy footsteps were the response this time, and finally the door opened, but it wasn't Frankie on the other side. It was a teenage boy in a Star Wars ringer tee hanging loosely on his chest and a backward ball cap on his head. Pretty much the last person Lily expected to find.

"I was looking for Frankie." Duh. She'd knocked on Frankie's door. Of course that was why she was there. She shifted the flowers again. "Is she home yet?"

The kid looked her over head to toe. Scrutinizing her flowy off-the-shoulder top, ripped jeans, and cowboy boots like he was the guardian of the gate. When he met her gaze again it was with a questioning squint. "You're Lily Lancaster, right? Are you Frankie's girlfriend or something?"

Or something sounded about right, but replying with *well, we've slept together a few times* didn't quite feel appropriate. Girlfriend. Why would the kid jump to that conclusion? She tightened her grasp on the bouquet in her hand. Oh yeah, that. "No, no. Just a friend."

The answer must have passed the sniff test. The teen shrugged. "Frankie usually doesn't get home until closer to five thirty, but I guess you can come in and wait." He stepped aside to let her through. "I'm Jake. I'm just here to clean her fish tank. You can, uh…" He shrugged again. "Whatever."

Jake shuffled his Converse back to the tank and the five-gallon orange bucket, and fidgeted with the plastic hose connecting the two, clearly unimpressed to find himself in the presence of Lily Lancaster. She dropped the bouquet on the breakfast bar between the kitchen and living room and helped herself to a glass of water from the tap.

Hanging out in Frankie's apartment filled Lily with the same sense of comfort she always had in her presence. The kitchen had the same shabby-chic vibe as the rest of the place with its vintage barn wood planks refashioned into cabinet doors and the tall, weathered stools at the bar. She hitched her hip up on one of the chunky butcher-block seats and grabbed the magazine from the basket on the countertop. It was an issue of *Country Weekly* folded open to an article listing the top ten rising stars in country music to watch for in the New Year. Lily was familiar with it—she recalled the photoshoot and interview that came with being appointed as number four. The New Year still seemed so far away even though it was nearly two weeks into December. It didn't even feel like it was time for Christmas to be rolling around yet. It was hard to feel like sleigh bells should be ringing when the sun was constantly shining so damn brightly. In some ways it felt like time in the outside world was standing still while she was in Las Vegas.

Lily hadn't realized how lost in her thoughts she'd become until she glanced up and saw Frankie standing in the living room grinning at her.

"You caught me," Frankie said with a sheepish expression. "I was studying up. That's a gorgeous photo of you by the way."

Lily's cheeks flushed hot at the compliment. "Such a ridiculous piece though. Angela wrote all of my answers."

Frankie's face scrunched up with disgust. "You mean none of this is true?" She poked a finger at the third paragraph. "Not even that one?"

"Nope. Angela made me say my favorite ice cream flavor is Rocky Road. Truthfully I prefer plain old chocolate, but she said that was too 'pedestrian.'"

"That woman is a real piece of work. There's nothing wrong with plain old chocolate." Frankie sidled up to the counter next to Lily and bumped shoulders with her. Her eyes sparkled with delight. "You know, even after a full day on the PR treadmill you still smell like cherry blossoms and sunshine. Are you sure you don't have time to grab dinner?"

She shook her head sadly. "As much as I'd love that, I used the little time I had for dinner to come here. I've got to get back to the hotel and get dolled up to perform at a fundraiser. It's actually a really good cause—they're a group that provides therapeutic horseback riding at summer camps for at-risk youth."

She laughed as Frankie drew back and raised a questioning eyebrow to her. "I didn't make that up. It's really a thing."

"I believe you. No one knows the healing power of interacting with animals more than I do."

"Um, excuse me." Jake cleared his throat. "I'm done with the tank." He held out his orange bucket as if offering proof.

Frankie stepped away and fished her wallet out of her purse as she escorted the teen to the door. "Thanks, Jake. See you next time."

He gave a friendly smile and wave as he left, shutting the front door behind him.

"He seems like a nice kid."

"He really is." Alone at last, Frankie took Lily's hand and led her to the couch. "Now please tell me what was so important that you used up your dinner time to come tell me it in person."

Warmth from their connection spread through Lily as they cuddled together. She would happily give up dinners forever if it meant she could have more of the rush when she touched this woman. Frankie didn't seem to be upset about their hijacked Rodeo Row date the day before, but Lily wanted to make sure her regret for how it went down was clear. Plus, she was excited to share what she had up her sleeve. "I came over here to apologize for yesterday."

"You apologized last night." Frankie waved a dismissive hand. "I understand it's your job. So let's leave that in the past. Besides, we had a blast at Rodeo Row. We might make it an annual event for us."

It was a relief to hear that the group enjoyed themselves, but it made Lily's heart ping with sadness that she had missed out. Another sacrifice. She very rarely got to hang out with friends. She'd been so worried that her absence had impacted Frankie's enjoyment that she hadn't stopped to consider her own loss. Either way, Frankie was right—they needed to leave any regrets in the past and move forward. "I also came to invite you to dinner tomorrow night, my treat. I've already made a reservation at Failte in the Emerald Isle Casino and ordered a car for us so please say yes."

"Yes." A beautiful smile split Frankie's face and Lily's heart soared again knowing things were good between them again.

"Great." She smiled back before leaning in to kiss Frankie squarely on the lips. "It's a date."

"So this was the important errand you just *had* to run this afternoon?"

Lily squinted into the makeup mirror to get a look behind at what Angela was worked up about this time. The small makeshift greenroom for the fundraiser's performers was devoid of artwork or anything that could absorb sound, so her manager's harsh tone was especially annoying. She was not about to let Angela kill her preshow buzz. "Whatcha got there?"

She hadn't been anywhere in public with Frankie, so there was no possibility that the paparazzi had caught anything regarding their gal-pal status, or relationship, or whatever the online journalists were calling it these days. Despite Angela's swift steps across the room while holding up her damn tablet yet again, Lily continued to fuss with her false eyelashes, making sure she was performance-ready for her turn on stage. She was one of several country acts appearing that night to promote a Rodeo Week concert. She needed to be at her best and grab as much attention as she could.

"What I've got is you on some kid's social media." Angela's sharp staccato grabbed Lily's attention as did the image on the conference table.

It was Frankie and her, arms wrapped around each other on Frankie's couch just a few hours before. A completely private moment in a completely private space. Nobody had even seen them together except…that little twerp! She cringed. Mr. Teenaged Fish Tank Cleaner wasn't so sweet after all. He must have snapped the pic of them through the window after he left the apartment.

"Did you read the post?" Angela continued before reciting it word for word. "Hanging with my neighbor and her girlfriend. Hashtag Lily Lancaster. Hashtag lesbos. Hashtag get some. Hashtag give it to her."

Lily bit the inside of her lip to keep from laughing. Clearly Angela didn't think there was anything funny about the situation but *get some* was so damn far off the mark of what had happened that it was downright hilarious. Angela's reaction was a little too mountain-out-of-molehill. "At least we avoided the paparazzi this time. It's just some kid's social page. How did you even find that?"

Angela blinked twice at Lily as if she thought she had completely lost her mind. "I have an intern whose entire purpose at the firm is to fetch coffee and check hashtags. That's not the point."

"It's one kid's social. His grandmother lives in the same building as Frankie. He's not even really a neighbor." Lily shook her head dismissively while tossing item after item back into her makeup bag. She was out of patience with the discussion. "Who even cares?"

"Your fans would care, and if you want to keep those fans you better start caring too." She snatched Lily's makeup bag out of her grasp, forcing her to focus on her point. "I am done fooling around on this subject. I forbid you to be seen with that woman in public again."

"You forbid me?" When did Angela become some kind of overbearing parent? Didn't *she* work for Lily? She planted her fists on her hips and puffed out her chest. Supergirl style. "That's not gonna happen."

Not to be moved that easily, her manager crossed her arms in front of her chest and leaned back against the edge of the conference table. "Oh yes it is."

The women stared at each other, unblinking until Angela caved, sighing as her arms dropped to her sides. "Can you please be a professional about this? It's nothing personal. It's not about Frankie."

"It sure as hell feels personal." Lily scrubbed her hands over her face. She had promised Frankie a fancy dinner to make up for blowing her off at Rodeo Row. She couldn't blow off that date too. "I've already made reservations for us at Failte tomorrow night. I owe Frankie a special night and I'll be damned if I'm not going to give it to her."

Angela winced at the phrase and Lily immediately regretted her choice of words. *Hashtag Give It To Her.* "Look, how about a compromise?"

Anything was better than letting Frankie down again, but Lily knew better than to agree blindly to one of her manager's deals. "What kind of compromise?"

"What if we switch your dinner to a more private venue?"

Lily shook her head adamantly. She could see where this was going. "I'm not agreeing to sorry-ass take out in my hotel suite if that's what you're suggesting. I promised her fancy and fancy is what I'm going to..." She chose her words more carefully this time. "Deliver."

"I'm thinking much bigger than that." Angela gestured wildly with her hands, a tell that she was over-selling an idea. Still, Lily was intrigued. "We'll bring in a chef. It might not be the chef from Failte, but we'll go big. And I'll talk with the manager about finding a location on the premises that is private yet perfect. How do you feel about dining under the stars?"

CHAPTER TWELVE

"So tell me about this mystery date," Mara said as she slipped a red checker into the yellow plastic grid. It slid into place with a satisfying click. "Did Lily tell you why she's keeping the location such a secret?"

Frankie tapped a black checker on the table and bit her bottom lip, more concerned with her next move than answering the question. Mara was famous for using distraction as a strategy for victory while playing board games. It was the same story every time they chaperoned the after-school game club at the LGBTQ Youth Center. She teased, joked, and distracted her way to beat her opponent. This time Frankie wouldn't break her focus. "No secret. She wants to surprise me. It's sweet and fun, and I'm excited about it so don't rain on my parade."

"I'm not raining on anything. I just think it's weird that one minute you've got reservations at one of the hottest restaurants in town and the next it's a top-secret table for two, God knows where."

"I can't help but notice your fixation on the word 'secret' here." Frankie dropped her checker into the slot and immediately winced at the result. She had fallen for Mara's tactics again.

"Connect four!" Mara's arms shot up victoriously above her head before her expression sobered. Her voice was a harsh whisper as she recovered. "I'm fixated on it because Lily is a lesbian but it's a *secret* and I think she's treating you like a *secret* too and as your best friend I want better than that for you. You deserve better than this kind of low-key love."

Frankie sucked in a breath and leaned back in her molded plastic chair. Mara's admission wasn't exactly a revelation. She'd been making snide comments to that effect ever since the group learned the truth about Lily and her arrangement with Brayden Judah. The big kiss in front of fans at Rodeo Row hadn't done anything to help either. More than once that week Frankie had to remind herself the comments came from a place of caring. Mara had not laid her opinion on the subject out on the ugliness table as plainly as she did in that moment, so Frankie had always managed to push her concerns aside. Fortunately, distraction worked in Frankie's favor this time as two teens approached hand in hand.

"Hey, Frankie," Grace said as she and Katie bounded up to the table. "I thought you were bringing Lily with you today."

Mara hit the release on the game, sending checkers skittering all over the table. While the girls giggled and tried to catch them before they hit the floor, she raised a smart eyebrow at Frankie.

Frankie's heart ached. She had thought Lily was going to be there too—at least that was the original plan. They were going to volunteer together at the center, but at the last minute Lily texted that she had some preparations to handle for their date and she wasn't able to make it. Frankie had thanked her lucky stars that she hadn't mentioned to Mara that Lily was going to join them at game club. It wasn't hard to regard Lily's no-show as proof of her avoidance of all things LGBTQ. Based on Mara's grimace, there was no doubt that was how she saw it now.

"Something came up and Lily said she'll have to take a rain check on game club." Frankie didn't dare look at Mara. She didn't want to see her smug look. "I'm sure she'll come another time."

"I hope so." Grace grinned and deposited a handful of checkers back on the tabletop. "I liked her. You like her, right? I mean, you *like her* like her, right?"

Keeping the smile from spreading across her face was a losing battle for Frankie. Her true feelings were bubbling over, and she needed to rein it in. She hated being less than honest with the kids, but she had to respect Lily's boundaries. "We're just good friends."

"All right you two." Mara shut down the conversation. "Why don't you go see if Jenna's got the snack ready? She can always use some extra hands putting it out on the table."

As the girls ran off, Frankie put the game away. If she kept herself busy enough maybe Mara would stop giving her the side eye and they could run off to snack time without further comment too.

She was wrong.

"So first Lily stood you up for game club, and then she canceled your big night on the town?" Mara pressed her lips into a straight line that indicated she was not amused. "Come on, Frankie. You've got to see the writing's on the wall here."

"She didn't cancel anything," Frankie argued. Mara wasn't being fair. There could be a million reasons why Lily changed their reservations. Frankie had seen firsthand how nutty things could get when Lily was out in public. Her mind wandered back to that first night and the drunk dude grabbing at Lily in the lobby of the Rothmoor. She couldn't blame her for wanting their date to be a little more low-key, and it definitely wasn't Mara's place to be judging her either. "It's a change of venue, that's it. And tomorrow when I call you up and tell you about my fabulous date with Lily you are going to eat crow."

"Well that sounds…gross." Mara scrunched up her face and laughed. "I'd much rather eat crudités and some of Jenna's trademark trail mix. Snack's out. Let's press pause on this for now. I've said my piece. I've done my due diligence here."

Frankie wasn't certain she'd proven her point, but she was relieved to have put the conversation to rest for the moment. She wanted to focus on enjoying her night with Lily and if that meant ignoring Mara's cautionary words that was what she would do. She would shove them into a little box, duct tape it up for good measure, and push it into a distant corner of her mind. She could unpack it later if it was still begging for her attention. After her romantic night with Lily. Enjoying the time she had with Lily while she was still in town had to be her focus.

Frankie walked onto the elevator, pleased that nobody had followed her into the car. She needed the solo ride up to Lily's room to mellow her mind. She ran her hands down the light fabric of her vintage boho dress. When they had spoken earlier Lily still wouldn't tell her where they were going, only that there would be dinner and she could dress casually. The long, bright floral-print dress paired with chunky espadrilles fit that bill.

It wasn't really the wardrobe selection or the date location that had Frankie's head spinning. It was more the wrestling match between her heart and head, and possibly a couple of other parts, regarding what to do about this relationship in which she had found herself with Lily. There was no denying the chemistry between them, but with Lily in Vegas for only two days more it made sense that Frankie should start to cool her jets and prepare to go back to life without her.

Only there was a little part of her that whispered long-distance relationships can work. Lots of people had done it. Penny and Lauren had managed to work through distance until Lauren was able to move from Chicago for them to be together permanently. Although Frankie wasn't thrilled at the prospect of moving to Tennessee to be with Lily, she was willing to do all manner of things for true love. If that was what this turned out to be, of course. That was just the way her hopeful heart was built. And with Lily's line of work, she could probably live anywhere. Maybe she would be willing to relocate to Las Vegas. Hell, they could live anywhere they wanted provided Frankie could find employment. The Clark County Animal Shelter didn't keep her feet planted in Vegas.

Beyond all that, Mara's warnings about getting involved with someone still firmly in the closet whispered doubt from a box in the far corner of her mind. She understood that Lily had made a promise to Brayden to work together for Rodeo Week, and she certainly could appreciate her loyalty to her best friend. But was coming out as a lesbian as detrimental to Lily's career as her manager claimed? And if so, would Lily really be willing to make that sacrifice? Would Frankie want her to?

The elevator's ding announced she had arrived, bringing Frankie out of her heavy thinking and back to the moment. She didn't want to spend the remaining precious time with Lily overanalyzing the situation. For all she knew Lily wasn't even thinking about the long term for them. Maybe it was just a here-and-now thing between them anyway. Frankie had to be able to accept that. She resolved to enjoy what she had while she had it, took a deep breath, and stepped out of the elevator.

When Lily greeted her at the door looking nothing short of stunning in dark-wash jeans, strappy silver heels, and a slinky hot pink tank top, the last wisps of worry in Frankie's brain dissipated.

"You look beautiful." She kissed Lily's cheek. Lily's cherry-blossom scent gave Frankie a heady rush, leaving her slightly dizzy as if suddenly under a spell. That was what it was like when she was in Lily Lancaster's orbit—the pull of attraction was just too great to even consider turning back.

"You do too." Lily took her by the hand, pulled her into the suite, and led her to the sofa. "Before we go to dinner I have a gift for you."

"A gift?" Frankie sat and fussed with her dress, arranging the fabric around her legs. She had showed up empty-handed and Lily was not only treating her to dinner, she was giving her something too. "You didn't have to do that."

"I know I didn't, but I wanted to." A coy smile spread across Lily's face. Delight in treating her to something special. "It was the least I could do after messing up our afternoon at Rodeo Row."

Excited, Frankie took the small box Lily passed her. She had a pretty good guess what it contained even as she lifted the lid, but she gasped just the same when she saw the delicate turquoise necklace she had considered buying at Rodeo Row. She was genuinely touched by the gesture. "You remembered."

"I wanted to give you something special so you wouldn't forget me when I head back to Tennessee. When I saw you looking at it the other day I knew it was perfect for you."

"Lily." Frankie ran her hand tenderly down Lily's bare arm. "I'll never forget you. But this is special and I appreciate it very much. Will you put it on me?"

Frankie sat still while Lily fastened the clasp around her neck, but the moment the necklace was in place she pulled Lily against her. She wrapped her arms around her and kissed her hard on the lips.

When they finally parted, Lily brushed her thumb along Frankie's jawline. "I really don't want to press pause on this." Her voice was thick with lust. "But we're late for dinner, and I kind of have something special planned for that too."

"Another surprise?" As the smile spread across Frankie's face, Lily traced it with her fingertip. Frankie's chest filled with warmth and her nipples went hard under the thin fabric of her dress. "What did I do to deserve the royal treatment?"

"Oh, probably lots of things." Lily grinned back as she pushed herself up off the couch and offered her hand to pull Frankie up too. "But truthfully I just like spoiling you."

"A girl could get used to that."

"Good. Now let's get to dinner. I'm starving." Lily led her out of the suite, not letting go of her hand the whole way to the elevator bay.

Frankie reached for the down button, but Lily stopped her with a light yank on her arm. "We're going up, not down."

"Up?"

"Yep." Lily wiggled her eyebrows mysteriously. "That's part of the surprise."

Frankie bit her bottom lip as she stepped into the elevator car. She was busting with curiosity, but it was clear from the twinkle in Lily's eyes that she was enjoying being the surpriser as much as Frankie was enjoying being surprised and she didn't want to ruin that for her.

When the elevator doors opened again onto the roof of the building, Frankie's breath caught in her throat. Lily's surprise did not disappoint. An ivory-colored canvas canopy was lit by a string of hanging bulbs illuminating a gorgeous table set with crisp white linens and crystal glassware. It was surrounded by floral arrangements in varying shades of purple, and potted ferns making it a private hideaway from the otherwise barren brick and steel rooftop. A waiter stood at the ready next to the table. He gave a slight nod as the women approached, then pulled out each of their chairs for them to sit.

"You did all this for me?" Frankie asked, slightly breathless from the shock of discovering the rooftop paradise. It was so beyond what any woman had ever done for her on a date that she wasn't sure whether she wanted to laugh or cry.

One of the happy consequences of the Rothmoor Towers not being the tallest building in Las Vegas was that the neon lights of the surrounding establishments flashed and twinkled all around them, casting a magical glow on their cozy rooftop tablescape.

Lily's creamy complexion absolutely glowed in the soft lighting as she beamed back at Frankie. She looked like an angel. "I did. I told you I wanted tonight to be special."

The women were quiet for a moment while the waiter filled their champagne flutes from the bottle chilling in the free-standing ice bucket beside the table. Every detail oozed elegance. Clearly no expense had been spared while making this special night come together.

Once he had stepped away, giving them privacy, Lily continued, "I wanted to give you an elegant, romantic night, but I also wanted it to be just the two of us. We're running out of time before I leave Las Vegas, so I thought I could squeeze both things into one night."

"I'd say you accomplished that." Frankie nodded and reached for her champagne. She held it up in a toast. "To my beautiful date. Well done."

Lily took a sip, then pressed her lips firmly together as if choosing her words carefully. "Also, there's something I want to talk to you about."

Frankie swallowed down her mouthful of champagne hard. "That sounds serious."

"It is, I guess." Lily reached across the table and grabbed her hand. Her touch was soft, but solid and reassuring. "But maybe not in a bad way."

The waiter returned to the table with salads and a silver basket of bread. Frankie glanced at Lily as she reached for the still-warm loaf. She suspected bread was not normally served with this type of meal, but rather another extra touch added just for her. She tore off a crusty chunk, releasing the yeasty aroma of freshly baked goodness. "You're trying to butter me up. Literally."

"Maybe." She conceded as she laughed at the joke. "I made a stop at that bakery you told me about. That place is off the hook! It felt like I'd stepped into a Parisian boulangerie. The whole place smelled like butter."

Frankie moaned. "God, I know. You should taste their croissants."

"I did," Lily stage-whispered with a playful wink. "Let's eat. We'll talk about the maybe serious thing after."

Despite her curiosity, Frankie agreed and resigned herself to enjoying the meal and the moment.

Lily took one last bite and leaned back in her chair satisfied. She had to hand it to Angela, she'd really come through for her this time. Chef Sebastian had grilled skewers of portobello mushrooms, chicken and vegetables and served them over lemon rice with a creamy yogurt sauce drizzle. It was delicious and sexy, and a wonderfully romantic meal. She swallowed the last of her wine and the moment she set the empty glass on the table the waiter stepped forward to refill it. The service all evening had been top-of-the-line.

Chef Sebastian approached the table. "Ladies, I have a fruit torte featuring fresh kiwi and berries chilling for your dessert. Would you like me to serve it now?"

"Thank you, Chef." Lily only took her gaze off her beautiful date for a moment to smile with gratitude at Sebastian. "I think we'll wait a bit before we indulge."

"Then I'll leave it for you to enjoy when you're ready. Have a magical evening." He bowed slightly before heading to the metal doorway that led into the building.

"That meal was amazing." Frankie pulled the napkin from her lap and shook the flaky breadcrumbs from it before laying it on the table, indicating she was satiated. "Thank you for a truly awesome date."

"It ain't over yet." Lily winked before addressing the waiter. "Thank you, Christian. We're good here."

The server nodded and set the bottle of wine on the table before leaving the same way as the chef.

With only the two of them remaining in the rooftop paradise, Lily made her move. "Why don't we head over to the cabana. The torte will keep." She stood up and offered her hand to Frankie.

They ducked through the curtains and sat side by side on the wicker lounger. The whole set up had been brought to the rooftop specially for their date. The interior of the cabana was lit with strings of fairy lights and the cushioned chair fit them both comfortably. Lily tugged the ottoman closer. They kicked off their shoes and put their feet up. She wrapped an arm around Frankie's shoulders. The night air had a chill and Lily pulled a fleece throw on top of them.

"This night keeps getting better and better," Frankie said with a contented sigh as she leaned her head onto Lily's shoulder.

"I've been longing to hold you like this again." She kissed the top of Frankie's head and boldly slid her hand up her thigh. She finally had a private moment with the woman she couldn't resist. She was totally prepared to make the most of it.

Frankie responded to the touch by reaching a hand up to Lily's hair, running her fingers through it to its fringed ends before trailing down her jaw line. When her fingertips came to rest on her lips, Lily nipped teasingly at them.

"Careful now." Frankie giggled. "I have teeth I'm not afraid to use too."

"Is that so?" Lily's voice dropped a register. It was suddenly hot and steamy—all worked up like the rest of her body. Frankie had that effect on her. She tipped her hand down to kiss Frankie's full lips and slid her hand up from her thigh to her breast.

The low moan that escaped Frankie sent a shiver up Lily's spine. "But, babe, what if someone comes up here and sees us?"

Lily shifted on the lounger, rolling on top of Frankie and pressing their bodies together. "Then they're going to get one hell of a show." She pressed her lips to Frankie's mouth before kissing her way down her neck to a favorite delicate place on her clavicle. By the way Frankie twitched beneath her, the magical spot still worked. Lily continued the journey along her skin, pulling the strap of Frankie's dress down over her shoulder as she went.

"I think I'm okay with that." Frankie's fingers tangled in Lily's hair again, guiding her lover to her chest. When Lily sucked a pert nipple between her lips, she gasped. "And I'm really okay with *that*."

Her reaction caused a buzzing in Lily's core. It was always like that when she was with Frankie. She got a charge knowing she was pleasing her and every gasp, every moan, every ragged breath only made her want more. She pushed the fabric of Frankie's dress out of the way, working her hands underneath it to connect with the soft skin of her upper thigh.

Frankie squirmed beneath her, then pulled her up for another kiss, this one long and deep. The fairy lights twinkled around them, adding to the magic of the evening. "Seriously, those guys aren't coming back, right?"

"Babe, I paid them handsomely and gave them strict instruction to stay the hell away once dinner was over." She read the silent question on Frankie's face. "And Rothmoor security will ensure we remain alone up here. It's all been handled. Promise."

"Good." Frankie peeled Lily's tank top off her. Because I need to feel your skin against mine. I need to have you right here on this rooftop couch."

Something deep inside Lily tugged downward and her pussy clenched with anticipation of Frankie making good on her words. If she wasn't wet before, she sure as hell was now. She shimmied her jeans down over her hips while Frankie wiggled out of her dress. Her eyes ran down the length of Frankie's beautiful curvy figure clothed only in a little blue lace thong. The waiting was more than she could stand, but before she could make a move, Frankie grabbed her by her bra—right between her tits—and yanked her back down on top of her.

"God, you are so sexy." Lily brushed her fingers over the flimsy fabric of that sexy blue thong and swallowed hard, her excitement building. "And wet."

She wouldn't wait another minute to take her. She kissed Frankie hard on the mouth, pushed the lace aside, and pressed two fingers into her.

Frankie gasped again as she adjusted to taking Lily in. As she began to rock along with the slick thrusts, Lily added another finger, filling her up.

"Just like that." Frankie's sultry whisper in her ear caused another jolt of pleasure in Lily's heat. "Make me come."

Lily increased the speed of her thrusting, brushing her thumb over Frankie's clit with each stroke. She stopped kissing Frankie long enough to watch her face as her body crested with pleasure. Her eyes rolled then fluttered closed and her lips formed a silent 'O.' Finally when Frankie squeezed her fingers, Lily stilled her hand and kissed her again, plunging her tongue into her mouth.

Frankie moaned, slow and satisfied, and yet another wave of bliss washed over Lily. She shifted her weight and rolled beside Frankie, snuggling into the crook of her arm. Her heart pounded like the baseline of one of her songs. This was what she'd been missing her whole life. This was the kind of thing she sang about. She had her music. She had her rising stardom. But this contentment and sheer joy at merely being cuddled up and connected in the way that she was with Frankie—that gave her a greater high than all the cheers and applause in the world. Who knew what would come next for her in the music biz? Maybe being out of the closet really would fuck it all up. But maybe what she felt when she was with Frankie was worth it.

She closed her eyes to breathe deeply and steady her racing thoughts. Frankie's usual citrus fragrance now mingled with the musk of sex. The combination was absolutely intoxicating. When she opened them again, she found Frankie grinning at her. "Why the face? What's that look for?"

"I could ask you the same thing." Frankie giggled and traced a fingertip along Lily's lower lip. "You look stoned."

She wasn't stoned, but she had a sneaking suspicion about what was floating her Zen. She had been wanting to talk this over with Frankie all evening, and the time felt more right than ever. Before she could overthink it, she let the words tumble out. "I don't want us to end when my gig in Vegas is over. Frankie, I want you to be my girlfriend."

Heaven. Frankie had entered the elevator in the Rothmoor Towers Casino lobby and ended up in heaven. That was the only explanation for it. She leaned back into the lush lounger cushions and gulped air, her head was still dizzy with pleasure. First Lily gave her what might have been the best orgasm of her life, and now she was asking her to be her girlfriend. The evening had been full of surprises. As she held Lily in her arms, she thought her heart might explode from sheer joy coursing through her veins. Passion was a powerful elixir.

This was the feeling she'd been seeking for so long. Lily had ignited her passion like no one else had in a long time. She was no more ready to give it up than Lily was. But still, there was that tiny voice in the back of her brain murmuring Mara's warning that Lily wasn't ready to come out. She wanted to ignore it, but she couldn't. "What about Brayden?"

Their gazes remained locked as Lily shook her head. "I'm ending that. I can't do it until after Rodeo Week because I already committed to that, but then it's over. Brayden and I will stage a breakup and that will be that. Frankie, you're the one I want to be with."

Relief flooded Frankie. The publicity stunts and fake dating with Brayden were going to stop. For good. Lily wanted to be with her. She wanted Frankie to be her *girlfriend*. Lily had said the word out loud. A word that had been music to Frankie's ears because it was more than just a random utterance. It was proof that Lily was serious about being with her. An aftershock of the orgasm hit her and her pussy squeezed again.

She placed her hand gently on Lily's cheek and her palm registered the contour of her smile. Lily's long eyelashes tickled the tip of her middle finger. Her heart jumped with hope as she looked into those earnest blue eyes gazing back at her. She couldn't deny she was falling for the beautiful woman beside her. If nothing else, Frankie owed it to herself to give a relationship with Lily a chance. "I'd like that. I'd really like to be your girlfriend."

With no more words between them, Frankie flipped their positions, climbing on top of Lily and kissing her urgently on her bright pink lips to seal the deal. "Now I'm gonna make you come until you're weak in the knees, *girlfriend*."

Lust flashed in Lily's eyes as Frankie slid down between her legs to make good on her words.

CHAPTER THIRTEEN

"I am going to move this stack and put it right here on top of this other stack next to your monitor. Is that okay?" Mara didn't wait for Frankie's answer. To Frankie's dismay, she cleared off the corner of the cluttered desk, hitched her hip up onto it, and settled in. Apparently she wasn't going anywhere until she had the conversation she had specifically stopped by the office to have.

Frankie sighed, dropped her pen on the papers in front of her, and slouched back in her chair frustrated with her endless paperwork. "It doesn't matter. I don't know if any of this matters."

"Aw, come on." Mara swung her legs back and forth over the edge of the desk like she didn't have a care in the world. There were no mountains of paperwork for comedians. "When you messaged me you were all excited to tell me about your big date last night. Don't let this crap get you down. Not until I get some dirty details anyway."

Frankie couldn't control the grin spreading across her face at the mention of her date with Lily, and she felt her whole body relax. Thinking about everything Lily had done to give her a special night put her right back on cloud nine. She was even able to ignore Mara's *dirty details* comment. "Oh, Mara, you should have seen it. Lily was absolutely gorgeous, dinner was delicious, and the—"

"Sex was hot as hell, right?" Mara finished with a pervy waggle of her eyebrows.

Frankie's cheeks flushed hot at the memory of some of their more intimate moments, but she wasn't about to disclose those specifics to Mara. "Yes, it was. But I was going to say the whole set up was so romantic. Like, completely out of a dream. Oh! And she gave me this." Frankie took the turquoise necklace in her fingertips to show it off.

Mara leaned across the desk to get a good look at the jewelry. "Mmmm, pretty." When she sat back up her brows pushed together and her expression darkened. "Expensive gifts, over-the-top dates—that's something."

"It *is* something." Frankie pushed herself up in the chair. Mara was obviously trying to make a point, but she was missing it. "Why does your face look like that?"

"I don't know." Mara shrugged her shoulders and examined her nails, avoiding eye contact. "It's just…" Her voice trailed off.

"Just what?" Frankie demanded. A dull ache was starting to develop at the base of her neck. Why was her friend trying to rob her of joy? "Lily gave me a super romantic night that felt good to me no matter what your misgivings might be. Please don't try to take that away from me."

"I'm not trying to take it away from you. You're my friend and I love you and I don't want you to get hurt." Mara dropped her hands in her lap and returned her full attention to Frankie. "I'm glad you had a nice date with Lily, and it sounds like she's working hard to woo you, but I can't help noticing that this big date occurred in a very private place where there was no chance of anyone seeing the two of you together. It's like she's hiding you away so she can stay in the closet and I think it's going to lead to nothing but heartbreak for you."

Frankie blew out a breath and leaned forward on her elbows, pushing her keyboard out of her way. She was blessed to have friends who looked out for her. She appreciated Mara's good intentions, but this time Mara was just plain wrong. "Lily and I discussed this last night. She asked me to be her girlfriend. *Her girlfriend!* We only have to make it through a couple more days of the act. Lily promised she would keep the performance with Brayden as low-key as possible until then. After that, she'll put an end to the whole pretending-to-date-Brayden thing. Things are going to change. You'll see tonight at the concert. Things are going to be different going forward."

Mara reached over and placed a kind hand on Frankie's shoulder. "If you're sure, kid. Like I said, I just want you to be happy. If you're good, I'm good." She gave her a little squeeze and shook her head to dismiss the subject and return to a tone more like her usual self. "Now seriously, what is going on with all these papers and files?"

Frankie groaned and let her head fall to the desk. "It's hell, Mara. It's fucking hell."

"Frankie, language!" Mara teased.

"I know. I'm sorry." Frankie mumbled against her desk calendar before lifting her head again. She had been more sweary than usual when it came to work lately. That wasn't a good sign about the state of affairs in her professional life. In the past week it had become pointedly clear: she had lost her passion for her work at the shelter. The realization made the necessary mundane tasks feel impossible. "I'm swamped with work and I don't know how I'm going to dig myself out."

She pushed her fingers into her hair and grabbed at her curls. It was the first time she'd admitted her frustration about her job out loud. She wasn't okay with the situation. She was plain unhappy with how her career was going. "I took this job because I wanted to work with animals and I know that all this administration shit is essential in the rehoming process, but it's no longer fulfilling. All these meetings begging companies for money and all the forms it takes whether the funds come in or not—it's exhausting. And when I think of this being it for the rest of my life—" She put her hands on either side of her head. "I want to scream."

Mara slid off the edge of the desk and held her hands out in front of her in a halting motion. "Please don't." She cracked a sad but sympathetic smile. "There's got to be a better way to handle it. What do you want to do as a career?"

"I don't know, but it isn't this." Frankie picked up a pile of manila folders and dropped them onto the floor beside her chair. By any chance do you need a sidekick in your act?"

"Not a chance. But I think I know what you need—at least for tonight." Mara grinned. "Your girl's only in town for another, what, forty-eight hours? You need—"

"Mara, I swear if that sentence ends with 'to get laid' I really am going to scream."

"Getting laid never hurts," Mara quipped. "But I was going to say you need to call it an early day here and come preconcert partying with us girls. We're all meeting over at Game of Flats to get this night started off right. You need to get out of here, get yourself concert-ready and get over there ASAP."

"Okay! I need to run back to my apartment and change first, but that shouldn't take me long. I don't want to miss any Game of Flats fun," Frankie said before giving her office a quick once-over glance. Truth was, the paperwork could wait another day and nobody would notice. Mara was right—Lily was only in Vegas for a little more than one day. Frankie needed to shake off the weight of the work week and carpe diem. "I'm in."

CHAPTER FOURTEEN

"Are you kidding me—we're having this conversation again?" Lily swiveled around in her dressing-room makeup chair to face Angela. "How the hell does this keep happening?"

"I don't know." Her manager frowned back at her. "How the hell does *this* keep happening?" She flipped her tablet around to point the screen in Lily's direction. Lily was really starting to hate that damn thing.

The headline read, "Lily Lancaster's Girl Gang," and underneath it was a picture of Lily, Frankie, and their friends sitting around a picnic table clinking their plastic beer mugs together at Rodeo Row. Also included were shots of Lily, Frankie, and Mara walking with arms linked, and one of the three of them jewelry shopping.

"Just some girls out on the town having fun." Lily shrugged. "I'm fun. I'm hip. That's a good thing, right?"

"Not when the caption reads, 'Lily Lancaster, her new gal pal, and lesbian comedian Mara Antonini.'"

"*Lesbian comedian* Mara Antonini," Lily repeated. "Why can't they just say comedian? What does *lesbian* have to do with anything?"

"That's how this game works, like I've been telling you." Angela stabbed her stylus at the screen again. "There are some words these people grab onto and *lesbian* is definitely one of them. I knew those hashtags from that kid's social media posts were going to bite you in the ass." She shook her head and blew out a breath. Not a hair in her strict bun moved with the motion. Hardcore. "In light of this incident, I think we can agree you have no choice but to do the dedication to Brayden tonight."

Lily groaned and slouched in her makeup chair. The paparazzi was totally out to get her. It just wasn't fair. "I sat with Brayden at that table for two freaking hours straight that day at Rodeo Row. Why didn't they get any pictures of that? Or from any one of the press events we attended after that?"

"Focus, Lily," Angela snapped with one final, emphatic poke at the tablet. "Do you know what you're going to say?"

Lily slipped out of her chair and paced in front of the mirror. She didn't know what she was going to say because she didn't want to say anything. She had attended Brayden's rodeo events, sat with him for autograph sessions, and even gone on the fake romantic dinner with him, but the dedication was one step too far. Not to mention she had told Frankie she was going to cool it with the Brayden crap when she asked her to be her girlfriend. It was time to stand up for herself and for Frankie. She spun on her heel to face Angela. "I don't want to do it. Frankie is going to be in the audience tonight and so are our friends—you know, my *girl gang*. What are they going to think if I get up on stage and make some fake-ass dedication to Brayden?"

Angela tucked her tablet under one arm and stood with the other hand on her hip. She was clearly prepared to stand firm on the issue as well. "They will think you are a person who takes their job seriously. Someone who keeps the promises they make to their very best childhood friend as well as their business manager."

Best childhood friend. Lily's heart sank at the thought of letting Brayden down. Angela sure knew how to pull her strings, but she had no one to blame for the situation but herself. She should have refused to go along with the whole ruse from the very start. Now she was stuck between the proverbial rock and hard place.

A knock on the dressing room door interrupted her thoughts. The stage manager poked his head into the room. "Thirty minutes, Ms. Lancaster. You've got a heck of a crowd out there excited to see you."

Lily thanked him and collapsed back into her chair. It was little comfort to know there was the Amphitheater full of people who were excited to see her when they didn't know the real her at all and, furthermore, probably didn't care to. "Fine, Angela. I'll say the thing. But would you at least find Frankie in the VIP section and give her a heads' up that I have to do the dedication to Brayden so she's not blindsided by it? Better yet, let me just write a quick note for you to deliver."

Despite the heat from a packed crowd dancing and swaying to the music, a chill of excitement shuddered through Frankie. She had always gotten a thrill from a live concert but attending a concert where her girlfriend up on the stage took her elation to the next level.

Her *girlfriend*. It had such a nice ring to it.

The night had started out with Frankie and her friends being escorted to the VIP section down in front of the stage area. Shortly after, Penny had stopped by amid her Production Manager duties to say hello and make sure the wait staff knew they were personal guests of both Lily Lancaster and the Rothmoor Tower Casino. From then on snacks were offered regularly and the drinks kept on flowing—a true first-class operation. By the time the opening act had cleared out and Lily took the stage the group was having a good time getting their VIP party on.

Frankie couldn't tear her eyes off Lily as she strutted across the stage belting out one of her more angsty, rocking country tunes about getting revenge on a cheating lover. Lily's cowboy boots stomped to the beat and she had just enough wiggle in her walk to draw Frankie's eyes to her ripped up blue jeans that were so tight-fitting they may as well have been painted on. Lily's choppy blond bob was fuller than normal, and even though she ran her hands through it and even tugged on it at one point during the song, her style held up.

The thing that really held Frankie's attention though was Lily's bright red lipstick. She stared mesmerized by that beautiful mouth, fondly remembering the delicious things it had done to her body the night before. A shiver of excitement worked its way down Frankie's core to pool between her legs. When Lily hit the high note to end the song and winked at Frankie as the drum pounded out the last beats, Frankie's nipples went rock hard. That smoldering look from her girlfriend was worth the price of admission. Her moment of sexual enchantment was cut short as Mara elbowed her in the ribs.

"I don't like the way that manager lady is looking at us," Mara shouted over the roar of applause. "She looks shady."

Frankie leaned forward and peered down the row past her friends to where Angela stood in the side aisle tucking a square of folded paper into her shirt pocket. Even at a country rock concert Angela wore her usual uniform: a business suit with her hair in a no-nonsense bun. Her arms were tightly crossed in front of her body and her expression was stoic. No cutting footloose for that woman. Frankie gave her a quick wave and Angela responded with a mirthless, tight-lipped smile that made her eyes turn to snake-like slits. Frankie turned back to Mara with a shrug. "Angela always looks like she's been sucking on lemons. That's just her way."

"Well I don't like it."

"Hush, Mara. Lily's about to say something." Frankie nodded toward the stage.

The audience quieted down as Lily approached the microphone. "How are you doing, Las Vegas?"

Another cheer went up from the crowd.

"I'm feeling good too." Lily's beautiful smile lit up her face. She oozed rock 'n' roll charisma as she addressed her fans. She straddled the stand and swayed her hips as she took the microphone in her hands. Her voice dropped to a lower, sexier register as she continued, "And this next song I want to dedicate to someone very special in my life. Someone who I can count on to be there for me, who loves me no matter what, and who fills my heart with constant joy."

Frankie's heart swelled at her country-music star girlfriend's words. All that Lily had promised about their future were coming true. The women were ready to move forward as a couple, and Lily was starting that transformation right in front of everyone.

Lily raised one hand in the air, a spotlight flashed on making her shine like a celestial being as the band played the opening measures of her song, "Bet On My Love." "Brayden Judah, this one's for you."

Frankie gasped as all the air was sucked out of her lungs. *Had Lily really just dedicated a love song to someone else?* She turned to ask Mara if she had heard the same thing, but words didn't come as another kerfuffle on the stage made the audience go crazy all over again.

Striding out into the spotlight straight toward Lily with a bouquet of roses and waving to the crowd like he had just been crowned prom king, was Brayden Judah.

Frankie caught the look of surprise that crossed Lily's face right before Brayden took her in his arms and kissed her long and hard to the delight of the crowd. Frankie's knees buckled and she collapsed into her seat. This was real. Very, very real. She swallowed hard against the lump rising in her throat as her brain struggled to make sense of it all.

"Frankie, are you okay?" Mara was by her side in a flash, holding Frankie's hand and pushing some wild strands of hair off her face.

Since the day Frankie met Lily there had been this fake relationship agreement with Brayden. She knew that. She'd even seen them interact, not that she had enjoyed witnessing it, but she had survived. But after the night she had shared with Lily not even twenty-four hours before, after all the words they had uttered to one another, after all the loving glances and lustful touches, seeing Lily lip-locked with Brayden Judah could quite possibly do her in. Her heart pounded as she wiped her sweaty palms on her skirt. Was there a hippo sitting on her rib cage?

"Frankie?" Mara put her hands on Frankie's shoulders and shook her. "Frankie, can you hear me?"

The noise of the crowd had become muted in Frankie's ears as if she were enclosed inside a bubble. Lily there on stage with Brayden was a total one-eighty from what the women had discussed the night before. Is this what a relationship with Lily Lancaster would mean—one more time for her career, one more time for the press, one more time for the fans? Always just this once…

"I can't do this," she gasped between rapid gulps of air. Mara had been right with all her warnings—Frankie had to be who she was, out and open. And watching Lily pretend with Brayden hurt too damn badly. Having a girlfriend who wasn't going to step out of the closet was not going to work.

"Frankie, what did you say?" Hayleigh was kneeling beside her with her hand on Frankie's thigh. Her big blue eyes were brimming with concern.

On stage, Lily finally launched into her next song—a country ballad about finding the love of a lifetime.

Frankie shook her head, struggling to find words. She had been starting to fall in love with Lily, and it wrecked her to think about letting her go, but she had to do it now before she was all in and the hurt was ten times worse. She couldn't be Lily's girlfriend if it meant going through this again and again. "I have to get out of here. I want to go."

Mara's expression shifted from worry to staunch resolution as she pulled Frankie up from her chair. She was strictly action. "That's it. You heard the woman. We're out of here."

Without requiring further explanation, the friends made their way down the row into the aisle. Jenna slipped an arm around Frankie's waist to guide her to the exit.

Angela stepped into the path of the group, eyebrows raised as if insulted by their hasty retreat. "Something wrong, ladies?"

"You can tell Lily we're going to pass on the after-party," Mara said simply before shouldering past the offended manager and ushering Frankie and the group out of the Amphitheater.

Lily kept her big, bright, girl-next-door smile plastered on her face through the encore, but the second the lights went down on the stage for the final time, she stomped through the wings and directly to her dressing room. Angela had taken things too damn far this time.

She had been completely blindsided by Brayden showing up on stage with that stupid bouquet of roses making a big scene out of kissing her and twirling her around. She'd played along because she knew that was what the fans wanted and she was too embarrassed to make waves, but the surprise had started a sickening pain in the pit of her stomach that had only worsened when she realized Frankie and her friends had all left the show shortly after the spectacle. She could only imagine the hurt she must have put Frankie through, and she had no idea how she could ever make things right with her.

She slammed the dressing room door closed behind her and collapsed into her makeup chair. Only then did she allow the tears that had been threatening as she left the stage to fall. She had given an inch with the dedication after Angela's last-minute guilt trip and her manager had taken a mile. She was angry with Brayden for going along with the stunt, but she had no doubt that Angela had been the mastermind behind it. Still, on top of the heartache of Frankie's disappearance, Lily was struggling with the sting of betrayal by her best friend. She was scowling at the reflection of her mascara-streaked face and wondering how she had let the charade with Brayden get so far out of control when her thoughts were interrupted by a knock on the door.

"Go away."

Angela entered regardless of her wishes. "It's just me. You were absolutely incredible tonight," she gushed. Could she not read the room? "I thought we could do a quick debrief before you head off to the after-party. By the way, your little group of friends said they weren't going to be able to make it. They left before your set was even done. Pretty rude."

Lily spun her chair around to face her manager. "I know they're not going to be there. I'm not an idiot. I saw them leave after the Brayden ambush."

"The Brayden ambush?" Angela batted her eyes innocently. "Brayden coming onto stage after your dedication was brilliant! Lily, the fans ate that up. It was the best thing you could've done out there. Just wait and see, your career is really going to start taking off after this. In a couple of weeks you'll be thanking me, mark my words. Now, come on. Let's get you changed out of your stage clothes and ready for the party. There are a lot of people who want to talk to you."

The only person Lily wanted to talk to wouldn't be anywhere near that party. Her throat burned and her stomach lurched violently as if she was going to be sick. How could she have done this to someone she cared so much about? She had to get to Frankie and at least apologize and try to explain. "Did you even give Frankie my note?" A glance at her manager's smug expression gave her the answer. "Forget it. No, I'm not going to the party."

"Don't be ridiculous, Lily. There will be reps from the label waiting for you, not to mention the press. They all want a piece of our star. And you need to give them that piece while they're hungry for it."

Lily slipped out of her chair and began to change her clothes, but she shook her head in response to her manager's directive. "They've taken enough of me. I have somewhere I need to be tonight and if the reps and the press don't like that, it's just too damn bad."

Angela's face went white, obviously shocked by Lily's defiance, but her voice remained even. "There's no choice here. You have to go to this party. Your career needs this."

Lily considered her manager's statement as she retrieved her bag from her locker and slung it over her shoulder. If she was going to lose something that night, she sure as hell knew what she didn't want it to be. She had to get to Frankie. "You know what, Angela? I don't care."

Without waiting for a reaction, Lily pushed past Angela and left the building.

It was a warm night for Las Vegas in December but Lily still wished she was wearing something heavier than the zip hoodie sweatshirt she had grabbed before running out of the Amphitheater to catch a taxi. She pulled it tighter around her body against the chill as she approached Frankie's apartment building. She dragged her feet across the sidewalk, questioning the wisdom in rushing over with no plan. She had no idea what she was going to say other than the honest truth and heartfelt regret. Frankie deserved that much.

As she climbed the stairs to the second-floor unit, memories of the other times she'd been there flashed through her mind. That very first night they'd hooked up, and of course, the fish-boy incident. Truthfully, she hadn't spent a ton of time there. A prickle of guilt traveled up the back of her neck. Things between the two of them had mostly unfolded on Lily's terms—and a lot of those terms had been dictated by Angela. Lily could see that clearly now. No doubt Frankie had too. Her shoulders slumped as she blew out a breath and knocked on Frankie's door.

"Who is it?"

Lily sucked in her breath and closed her eyes in silent prayer for the Hail Mary play she was about to attempt. "Frankie, it's me. Can we talk?"

The slide and click of the door being unlocked was the only response from the other side, but it was the sound of hope to Lily.

Lily fought her tears as Frankie leaned against the door frame, arms crossed. Unmovable. Her heart sank. This wasn't going to go well. She had to get what she had to say out before she got a door slammed in her face. "Frankie, I'm so sorry. I know how that must have looked, but I need you to know I had no idea that Brayden was going to come out on the stage. Absolutely none whatsoever. Angela set it up but didn't tell me because she knew I wouldn't stand for it."

"It looked like you went for it once he showed up." Frankie's posture was rigid and she continued to stand next to the door even after Lily stepped inside. She clearly had no intention of this being a long visit, but at least she let the door click shut keeping their conversation from being overheard by the neighbors.

"You know there's nothing between Brayden and me except for friendship. It caught me off guard when he showed up on stage tonight. I didn't know what to do and all I could think was *the show must go on*, so I went along with it. I know how it must have looked and how you must have felt."

"You have no idea how I felt." Frankie's voice rose and her eyebrows scrunched down on her forehead. Lily had never seen pain like that flash in her eyes before. "It hurt, Lily. It hurt because I was jealous that you were kissing someone else that way in front of everybody, and because you lied to me when you said you weren't going to continue to do that fake relationship stuff anymore. But on top of that, it hurt because I realized I can't be your girlfriend if it means being in the closet, and right now that's what it would mean. How could I work with those kids at the center and tell them to be true to themselves and then turn around and not be honest in my own life? I can't do it."

Lily's heart was in her throat. She had never meant to hurt Frankie. She had to know that. Desperately scrambling for the right words to fix things, she took a step toward her to close the gap between them. "Please give me a chance to make this right. I really care about you and now that Rodeo Week is over we can—"

"Stop." Frankie had tears in her eyes as she held out a hand to halt both Lily's motion and words. "I've heard this all before. My mind is made up. If I stay with you I'm only going to end up getting hurt more than I already am. You need to sort things out with yourself before you can start anything solid with someone else. I'm telling you this because I care about you too."

Anything solid with someone else. Frankie had taken them as a couple out of the equation all together. Lily's brain frantically searched for a response that would achieve what her heart wanted, but as the silence between them stretched she came up empty. Frankie was right. Lily wasn't being fair. She couldn't be a good girlfriend to anyone until she could be her authentic self. A tear slid down her face and dripped off her chin as she met Frankie's gaze one last time with a nod of acceptance. "I'm gonna go."

Without a word Frankie opened the door, but as Lily walked down the hall she heard her sad voice. "Goodbye, Lily Lancaster."

Frankie clicked the lock in place, shutting Lily out of her life. She leaned her back against the door to steady herself and let the tears she'd been holding in finally fall. This wasn't how the night was supposed to go. Her head was pounding and her heart still felt the agony of seeing Lily and Brayden on that stage together. The image was stuck firmly in her brain, its sharp, ragged edges digging in to become a permanent fixture. A lump of dread and grief built in her gut.

The initial shock and anger had faded by the time she'd arrived home from the concert. It was replaced by a residual hurt. Sadness at what she'd lost, what could have been. She scrubbed her palms over her face and pushed off the door determined not to dwell in self-pity. She'd been swept away in the whole girlfriend thing. Fallen under the spell of the romantic rooftop lighting on that special night with Lily. She'd been stupid with love and lust.

She ambled numbly to her bedroom and changed into boxers and an old threadbare T-shirt from her sorority's spring party her senior year. Dragging the comforter off her bed behind her, she made her way back to the living room and curled up on the couch in front of the television. Her heart clenched at the wave of emotion washing over her as she snuggled up on the blanket that still smelled of Lily's cherry-blossom perfume.

If only things could stay the way they were the night it all started. That night before Frankie even knew who Lily Lancaster the country-music star was. Before Brayden. Before Frankie's friends had all weighed in on the situation and the paparazzi started following them. Before all of it. When it was just the two of them—Frankie and Lily drinking beer and swapping stories at Game of Flats.

But that wasn't reality. Reality was that Lily was building a career, one she'd worked damn hard for, and Frankie had…well, she had a life that she lived proudly. Even if it did need a few tweaks in a big bad way. Heck, she'd made the Thirty Under Thirty list thanks to her innovations at the animal shelter. She had that feather in her cap. She just had to figure out her next step. The fact was, no matter in what direction Frankie's life went, it definitely wouldn't be back in the closet.

She tugged the blanket more tightly around her and cued up the first season of *Gilmore Girls* on her television. Letting Lily go was for the best. It was what made sense for the both of them. Now, if only her aching heart would get the memo.

CHAPTER FIFTEEN

It was Monday afternoon and Frankie was comfortable on her couch surrounded by the spreadsheets she had printed out. She had made it almost through season three of *Gilmore Girls* when there was a knock on her door. She had no intention of answering, but when Mara started yelling for her to open up, she began to worry about upsetting her neighbors and gave in.

"So, how are things going here?" Mara pinched the edge of an empty Veggie Chips bag and transferred it from the couch to the coffee table before sitting down. It was clear from the way she eyed up Frankie's sweatpants and tie-dyed T-shirt that she had concerns about the situation. She nodded in the direction of the television. "You called off work to write the great American novel and see if the Independence Inn stays afloat?"

Frankie sighed. How to explain? She was making a plan, but she was almost certain her friends would think she'd totally lost her mind this time. Over the past forty-eight hours she had acknowledged their texts with brief responses—enough to let them know she was okay, but she had suspected eventually one of them would surface in person. They had to have known they would find her on the couch watching her go-to comfort show. Now that Mara had actually made an appearance in her apartment she was going to have to take a leap of faith and let her in on her idea. Eventually. "Someone has to keep an eye on breaking Stars Hollow business news."

Her attempt at humor didn't fool her friend. Mara knew her well enough to know when something was up. She tugged on Frankie's arm until she gave in and tumbled onto her lap. Her fingertips raked through Frankie's curls as she spoke gently. "I know you're hurting. That's completely understandable. But missing work is so not you. Sweetie, we're worried."

Frankie could count on one hand the number of times she'd called off work at the animal shelter, and they were all for honest-to-God illness. She still felt the nip of guilt from lying that morning, but on top of what had happened with Lily, she couldn't find the strength to face that paperwork mountain. It was all too much. And once the inkling of an idea had taken hold in her mind, she'd become obsessed. She couldn't stop until she'd considered all the angles and determined if it was a legit possibility. Still, she hadn't meant to give the girls a scare. "I'm sorry, Mara. I just needed a day."

"I'm guessing you haven't heard from Lily?" Mara continued to play with Frankie's hair. This was the thing about Mara that had always impressed Frankie the most. The moments when she finally shed her class-clown exoskeleton and took a break from the jokes, she was the kindest, most loyal friend you could ask for.

"Nope. Lily Lancaster has left Las Vegas." Frankie sat up and took Mara's hand. She appreciated her friend's support, but she shook her head. It wasn't that she didn't still feel the sting of Lily's absence. Her body still ached with the memory of her touch and her heart felt as if a chunk had gone missing. Left town right along with the woman she had fallen for. But she still believed it was all for the best despite the hurt. She stood firm on the fact that she couldn't be in a relationship with someone who wasn't ready to be out of the closet. "I think maybe the timing was off for Lily and me. And honestly, I think I'm okay with that. She has her music career to work out, and I need to get some things sorted too."

Frankie had allowed herself that first night to sulk about losing Lily, but when she woke the next morning she realized there was more to what she was feeling than regret over their lost relationship. Lily had helped her see she needed to do something passionate with her life. Being in a relationship wouldn't solve that problem. After all the judgment she'd cast upon Lily about needing to find herself before she could be with someone else, here she was in the same boat. Or maybe a different *boat*, but in the same sea. Frankie needed to get herself together before she could be a good partner too. The only question was *how?* So Frankie had sat herself down and using a not-so-scientific mix of daydreaming and list writing she came up with an idea that not only sparked passion, but also seemed realistic and feasible.

Mara scrunched up her face trying to follow. "So you're not holed up in this retirement village watching this classic fast-talking dramedy because you're heartbroken about losing Lily Lancaster?"

"That's how it started, but not anymore. I just needed a couple days to reset." She shifted nervously on the couch and stretched her back straight, taking a deep breath before sharing her plan. *Here goes nothing.*

"I want to buy Café Gato."

Mara's eyes went wide and her jaw dropped like a cartoon character who's realized they'd run off a cliff and no longer have solid ground under their feet. "You want to buy Café Gato?"

"Uh-huh." Frankie nodded her head and swallowed hard. Saying the idea out loud to someone else was very different from figures on paper. Telling her friend about her plan felt very do-or-die, and that made her chest swell with excitement. With *passion*. "I'm hoping to draw in some investors, and I'll need to take out a loan of course, but I've worked it all out and I strongly believe I can do it."

Mara surveyed the mess of papers around them. She picked up one of the discarded lists and sucked her bottom lip between

her teeth as she studied it. Frankie always could trust Mara
to shoot from the hip. If she was going to classify her plan as
completely harebrained she wouldn't beat around the bush.
Frankie's pulse beat in her throat as she awaited the verdict. She
clenched and unclenched her fists until Mara's gaze finally met
hers again.

"If you believe you can do it, then I believe you can do it."
She gave a stiff nod before a wide smile spread across her face.
"And I assume when you say investors, you mean—"

"Yeah." Frankie eyed the paper in her friend's hand and gave
sheepish shrug. "We've talked them into doing weirder stuff
than this. Why not?"

A smirk crossed Mara's lips and just like that she was back
to her regular smart-ass self. "That is excellent news because
I came to drag you to Café Gato for happy hour and now you
have the perfect venue to present your idea to your potential
investors."

"Happy hour at the café?"

"Yep." Mara stood and clapped her hands as if expecting
Frankie to jump to attention. "Hayleigh's bringing her flask to
add a little 'happy' to everyone's coffee, so get your ass out of
those sweatpants, do something with that hair, and let's go."

"Seriously? *Do something with that hair?*" Same old Mara.
Frankie rolled her eyes to show she took offense but rose from
the couch as commanded.

Mara smacked her playfully on the ass. "Move it, kiddo. You
don't want to keep your investors waiting."

"Oh my God, you guys. Get over here." Hayleigh waved and
called out to Frankie and Mara as they stepped into Café Gato.
Apparently the Baileys was already flowing and the alcohol had
kicked in. As the women pulled chairs up to the table where
Victoria, Jenna, Hayleigh, Penny and Lauren were all sitting,
the excited blonde continued to fill them in. "Maeve just told
us—they have a potential buyer. But he plans to shut down the
café and do something entirely different with the space."

"No more Café Gato?" Frankie frowned.

"No more café anything," Jenna confirmed with a sad, tight-lipped nod.

"What's the new place going to be?" Mara asked as she gave a wave to Maeve at the counter.

"Some kind of junky retail space from what Maeve told us. Like an Everything Under Five Dollar Las Vegas Souvenir Shop." Victoria shook her head sadly. "Maeve and Zig hate that it won't be a café anymore, but they're ready to unload the property and get on with their retirement, so if the price is right on this offer—"

"Wait." Mara interrupted her girlfriend. "They haven't accepted an offer on it?"

"Not yet." Jenna shrugged. "But you heard what Victoria said. The deal is practically done."

"No, no, no." Frankie slapped her palms on the table, her frustration finally getting the best of her. After all her plotting, planning and scheming she was too late. This couldn't be happening. "I seriously cannot take it." She grabbed Hayleigh's flask of liquor and took a swig directly from it.

Maeve arrived at the table with coffee for the two newcomers. "You couldn't wait two more seconds, young lady?"

"Sorry, Maeve." Frankie tipped a second shot into the mug Maeve set in front of her before passing the flask to Mara.

"Don't be too hard on her." Victoria pushed the caddy of sweeteners across the table in Frankie's direction. "She just heard the news about the café and she's not taking it well."

"Oh, sweetie." Maeve stood behind Frankie and grabbed her by the shoulders, planting a motherly kiss on the top of her head. "I didn't know you were so upset about this. You've been so supportive of me and Zig. I didn't know the change would hit you so hard."

Frankie turned in her seat toward the older woman. "I am *so* happy for you and Zig and your retirement plans. Honestly. It's just that Café Gato has been *our* place for so long." She gestured at her friends around the table, surprised by the sting of tears. "I can't stand it. In fact"—her gaze moved around the table, looking at each of her friends in turn—"I was thinking about buying it myself."

A hush settled over the group as her words sank in, but then suddenly they all started talking at once.

"Are you kidding me?"

"Frankie, this would be perfect for you!"

"That's a great idea!"

"You have got to do this!"

"Hold up, everyone." It was Mara who called the group back to order as she set her mug back down with a loud clunk. "Maeve, you haven't actually accepted the offer yet, have you?"

Maeve's mouth puckered in concern as she shook her head. "Not yet, but—"

"Don't." Mara stopped her. "Frankie has a solid plan. We just need a little more time to work out a few details. If you can hold off accepting any other offers until we check into a couple things, Café Gato might just live to see another one of its lives."

"Oh, *cat. Nine lives.*" A tipsy Hayleigh giggled. "I see what you did there."

"Mara, we can't afford to miss out on what is a very decent offer." Maeve frowned. "We have other plans already in motion."

Mara's *couple of things* may have been an understatement. The real estate and business would need to be independently valued before the bank would even discuss a loan with Frankie, and she would need to examine the café's books, tax returns, property outgoings, turnover figures…she would have to work night and day to make it happen, but owning the café would be worth it.

"Just give me forty-eight hours," Frankie pleaded. "Please. I promise I can have it worked out by then."

Maeve glanced over at her husband who was wiping down the counter oblivious to the promise she was making. She sighed and nodded her agreement. "Okay. Two days, but that's it. You girls are something else. We're going to miss you." She gave them a warm smile and Frankie's shoulders one last squeeze before bustling off again.

The group at the table shifted in their seats to focus on Frankie. She sipped her coffee casually and blinked innocently back at them. "What?"

"Do you seriously want to do this?" Penny, ever the serious businesswoman, narrowed her eyes at her from across the table. "You're going to quit your job and buy the café?"

"She really does." Mara jumped in with a nod. "She made graphs about it and everything."

Frankie shot her a warning glance before addressing Penny. "I really want to do this. I've thought it all through. I'm ready for a change in my life and owning Café Gato is it. I…feel passionate about it."

"It makes sense," Mara chimed in. "Frankie's been unhappy at her current job and needs a change. Owning the café would still give her the opportunity to support the shelter since it's right next door." She turned to Frankie. "Hell, it would be super convenient to volunteer there if you miss your furry friends."

"This is brilliant and it *could* totally work." Victoria's eyes brightened as she latched on to her girlfriend's train of thought. "You would just be flip-flopping your situation now where you work at the shelter and help out over here."

"It's kinda perfect," Jenna agreed. "You already know so much about the café from helping Maeve and Zig."

"And you know about ordering supplies and keeping inventory from working at the shelter," Mara added. "What difference does it make if you're ordering coffee beans or dog chow?"

"Um, the woman does have a business degree too," Jenna said poking a know-it-all finger in the air.

Frankie chewed on her bottom lip as she struggled to keep her emotions in check. Sitting there in the café, it was easy to picture herself running it—serving coffee and sweets, chatting with customers, holding special events. Her heart soared. It had been a long time since she had felt excited about her career. Running the café would be a gamble, and stretch her financially, but it was exactly the kick in the pants her life needed now. A true passion project. She was still going to need some help from her friends if she had any hope of pulling it off. She would definitely need Penny to use some of her connections to get everything done under the forty-eight-hour deadline. She sucked in a deep breath and went for it.

"Actually, Penny, I was hoping you'd be interested in investing in the café. I know you're always on the lookout for good projects to jump onto, and what could be a better investment than real estate in Las Vegas?"

Penny leaned her elbows on the table and steepled her fingers in front of her face, tapping them together for a beat before speaking. Taking her time to think. "It's an intriguing offer. I'll want to check out the figures before I commit." She smiled. "But I'm sure we can work something out. I'll make some calls for you too."

A happy flutter rose in Frankie's chest. Suddenly, owning her own business was beginning to feel like a real possibility.

"You know, I wouldn't mind being an investor," Victoria mused as she got up to fetch the coffee pot from the burner behind the counter. "I have some available funds that could be doing better. I'd like to see the figures too."

"Me too." Mara grinned and held out her mug for a refill. "I mean, I've seen the spreadsheets and the lists. But I want to invest as well."

"And those of us without casino-heir money or famous-comedian money will pitch in around here however you need us," Jenna offered as she slipped an arm around Hayleigh's shoulders.

Frankie looked around the table at her friends. Her heart warmed with love for all of them and their willingness to support her when she needed it most. She couldn't hold back the smile that spread across her face as she threw her arms in the air like she had won the lottery, because with these friends it felt like she really had done just that. "Let's do this."

The others cheered, clapped, and hooted while Mara pounded on the table and exclaimed, "Hayleigh, pass around that flask again. We're celebrating tonight!"

CHAPTER SIXTEEN

"Aunt Lily watch me!"

"No, watch me!"

Seven-year-old twins Cadee and Travis called out from their backyard playset amid giggles as Lily and her sister Sarah sat on camp chairs by the firepit. As the sun set their antics had grown increasingly daring to the point where Cadee was hanging upside down from the monkey bars on the elaborate structure Lily had purchased for them the Christmas before.

"I am watching you both and you are fabulous stars in the area of playset gymnastics, but how about coming over here and sitting down for s'mores." She lowered her voice and added, "Before someone breaks a neck."

"Oh, Lily, they're fine. They do this kind of stuff all the time." Sarah waved a dismissive hand at the joyfully screeching kids as she reached into the cooler for a bottle of water. "We used to be just like them, only we didn't have a fancy Backyard Discovery Elite Set. We had hay bales and tree limbs. Oh Lord, remember the way you used to jump from the tire swing?" She chuckled.

"Yeah, we sure took our share of bumps and bruises. Now I'm hollering at your kids the way Mama used to holler at us." Lily shook her head and pulled her throw more tightly around her shoulders. It had been in the low fifties when they'd set up around the fire pit, but as the sun dipped on the horizon the temperature had taken a dive as well. The December chill didn't seem to impact the kids at all as they continued to play. "I've completely lost my backyard stunt cred. I'm just glad I remembered to pick up the helmets to go with the scooters."

"Speaking of which, you don't have to show up with expensive gifts like electric scooters every time you come back home. I have to live with those rug rats and you're setting standards I cannot possibly keep up with." Sarah's eyes sparkled with teasing as she passed Lily another beer.

"Those were early Christmas presents. Besides, I want to treat them while I still can." Lily blew out a breath and twisted the cap off her bottle. Christmas at home with her family was usually her absolute favorite season, but for some reason she hadn't quite got caught up in the spirit this year. In the past two weeks she had messed up a great relationship with a perfectly sweet woman, broken up with her best friend, and played fast and loose with her music career. Christmas was only a week away, but instead of joyful her heart felt heavy and sad. "I want to be their famous Aunt Lily while it lasts."

"You're being ridiculous on many levels, little sister. First of all, those two kids are wild about their Aunt Lily and will remain so whether she's a famous singer or not." Sarah adjusted herself in her seat to prop her feet up on an empty camp chair and spread her blanket over them. "But secondly, you're mourning a career that is very much alive and kicking. Hell, based on the gossip-rags' coverage of you the past two weeks, I'd say you're more popular than ever. Was there anything else even going on at Rodeo Week besides the alleged romantic drama between you and Brayden Judah?"

Lily groaned and took a large swig of beer. She had kept her sister in the general loop while she was in Las Vegas, but immediately upon her return to Bell Buckle she had filled her in on all the details, including how she had managed to find and lose Frankie Malone all in a span of a two-week trip and how her friendship with Brayden had crashed and burned. *Ugh. Brayden.* "Please don't even speak his name. I'm still mad as hell at him."

"Lil, Brayden is your best friend." Sarah frowned. "Yes, he may have been out of line blindsiding you on stage like that at the concert, but you know he was only doing it for his career like you had been doing right along with him all this time. How the two of you have managed to pull off this hetero-couple act for so long anyway is a mystery to me. If they would've seen the two of you as teenagers running around town together they might have an entirely different outlook on things."

In spite of herself Lily laughed remembering some of their antics as kids. Sarah was right. If people only knew about the many hours Lily and Brayden had spent in her bedroom choreographing dances to Kesha songs they might have given the subject a closer look. They would pretend that someday they would go bursting into their prom and perform their routine, possibly with classmates joining in like the big dance scene at the end of "Footloose." Of course, it was just a silly dream. In reality the chance that their display would have been met with the approval of their classmates was slim to none.

They weren't quite as lucky as those kids who had the Winter Formal at the LGBTQ center. *Ugh.* The prom made her think of Frankie and that fun night they had shared, and that just reminded her of how much she missed her. She'd really made a mess of things in Vegas. That much had become clear after returning home. "Yeah, I guess it's finally time to set everyone straight." A raspy, ironic laugh escaped her before she could bite it back. "So to speak."

"What are you going to do about it?" Sarah raised an eyebrow in her direction. A big-sister move she had perfected over the years.

"I have a meeting with Angela in the morning." Lily sighed and took another long swallow of beer. "I'm gonna tell her I've decided to be a lesbian instead of a country-music star."

"Lil, I'm serious."

"So am I."

Sarah pressed her lips into a thin straight line and studied Lily's face. An owl hooting in the distance and the swings creaking on the playset filled the otherwise silent air around them. "I don't see why it has to be one or the other—country star *or* lesbian."

Lily kicked the tip of her boot at the pavers outlining the firepit before surrendering with a sigh. "It has to be one or the other because my manager, Angela, said so."

"Why does Angela get to dictate what happens? This is your life. Your career doesn't have to be over because you're gay. It might change, sure, but hang on tight and ride the bucking bull. Figure it out. If Angela doesn't like it, then maybe it's time to get a new manager."

The twins running over to join them by the fire brought the conversation to a halt. Lily reached out an arm and Cadee climbed onto her lap and tucked herself under the blanket. Sarah had made a good point and as Travis handed around marshmallow roasting sticks, Lily considered her words. Why *did* Angela get to dictate what happened next?

Lily helped Cadee fix marshmallows on her stick. Angela had said it would hurt Lily's career if she ducked out of that post-concert party in Vegas and she had been wrong about that. In fact her album cracked the top ten on Billboard's country chart right afterward. As Cadee hopped down to get closer to the fire for toasting, Lily made up her mind. Why shouldn't she tell Angela she wanted both? At this point she had nothing to lose. She may as well ride the bull.

Two days later, Lily sat in Angela's Nashville office drinking coffee and bracing herself, ready to make her announcement. As much has she wanted to be Lily Lancaster: Country Superstar, she wanted to be Lily Lancaster even more. Who knew what impact coming out would have on her trajectory to stardom? The world could be an unkind place. It could all be downhill after this. In the end though, she knew it was worth it to find out.

She'd practiced many eloquent speeches to deliver that morning, but in the moment her words simply tumbled out, honest, brave, and amazingly freeing. "I'm not gonna hide who I am anymore. I'm coming out."

Angela leaned back in her chair and folded her arms. A cool, kind, knowing smile slid across her face and it was the prettiest Lily had ever seen her look. "I had a feeling that was what you were coming here to say. That's why I asked Van to join us. I can't manage your career if you're going to come out publicly, but not for the reason you think."

Lily's gaze bounced from Angela to the other woman smiling encouragingly and…tapping out notes on her tablet. *Was tablet tapping the key to good talent management or something?* But that was the only thing Van had in common with Angela. Van's style was much more relaxed—dark skinny jeans paired with a paisley-print button down rolled up to her elbows revealing a white thick-banded watch on her wrist. Her high-top Converse sneakers looked a lot more comfortable than Angela's stilettos. And her jet-black hair was styled in a sleek pompadour. Still totally professional, but much more modern than Angela's strict, no-nonsense bun.

"It's great to meet you." Van stuck out a hand to shake, exposing the rainbow-filled heart tattooed on her right wrist. "Angela's been getting me up to speed on what's been going on with your career, and I'm confident I can help."

The tension in Lily's shoulders that had plagued her all morning started to melt. She had a good feeling in her gut about Van. "It's good to meet you too, and I look forward to hearing your plan of attack."

"I'm really happy for you, Lily," Angela continued, "but I don't know how to be the best manager for you as a lesbian country singer. Luckily Van does. She has experience specifically working with LGBTQIA artists so she can handle your career with an expertise that I just don't have. Like I've said all along, I want the best for you. Oh! And Van's group has an office in Las Vegas, so that will be very convenient."

Las Vegas. Frankie's home. Angela thought it was all about Frankie. The sentiment was kind, despite being off the mark. "I'm not…I think I'll be staying here for a while."

Angela stared back blankly as if Lily's words didn't compute. "I'm sorry, I just assumed—"

"It's okay." Lily shook her head to dismiss the awkward moment. "I'll probably have my hands full with Van's plans for my career anyway, so hunkering down here at home is probably best for now."

Surprise registered on Angela's face as she rose from her seat, but good grace seemed to prevail as she excused herself. "Then I'll leave the two of you to the planning while I go get some more coffee."

Van shifted in her seat and focused her full attention on Lily. "I'm ready to get started if you are. I have a lot of ideas on how you can come out publicly but on your own terms. I've done this before with a dozen other budding celebrities. We can make this work."

CHAPTER SEVENTEEN

One week later, Frankie closed her eyes, took a deep breath, and pushed through the front door of Café Gato. *Her* café. The ink wasn't even dry on the papers that made her the owner, and the minute she got the keys she went straight there. She couldn't resist. Penny had pulled some strings with people her father knew to expedite the real estate deal and the renovations. More than strings. They were miracles really. Frankie's vision was coming together.

The constant hum of the walk-in fridge was the only sound in the café, but it was music to her ears. She clicked on the lights behind the counter and started the coffee maker. The dream began with a cup of joe in her very own café.

As the machine popped and whirred to life, she walked the floor and pictured the changes she wanted the contractors to make: a built-in bar for the sweeteners and creamers, a row of booths against the far wall, and some shelving for grab-n-go offerings.

Maeve and Zig had taken the art from the walls, leaving the place looking bare, but Frankie already had her own décor in mind anyhow. Jenna would be coming by later in the week to paint a brightly colored mural on the long wall where the new booths would be, and Penny's girlfriend, Lauren, had scheduled a photoshoot with some of the cats from the shelter to produce framed portraits to fill the blank spaces. The only thing the former owners had left behind was the bulletin board by the register, which Frankie planned to take down anyway. She could either stick it somewhere in the back office, or maybe they could use it at the youth center for something.

As she strode across the room to take it off the wall, she realized the takeout menu still tacked to it wasn't just any old menu—it was the one Lily had autographed the night of the poetry slam when they'd helped out at the café. That same night she'd taken Lily in her arms and danced her around the shop while Lily sang along to the radio. Maeve had probably left it as a reminder to Frankie of how happy she'd been that night. *Little did Maeve know then how that relationship would crash and burn.* Tears prickled at the back of Frankie's eyes as she grabbed the menu and tore it into tiny pieces that she dropped in the trash bin. Good riddance, country-music star Lily Lancaster.

She closed her eyes and inhaled deeply, immediately regretting the rash behavior. Her relationship with Lily hadn't worked out as she'd hoped, but it had taught her a lot nonetheless. She'd proven that she wouldn't compromise when it came to being her true self. And without her time with Lily she may never have realized this venture that would bring balance to her life. Maybe it was like that old country song Lily had introduced her to—something about unanswered prayers being a gift.

Penny knocking on the glass door pulled her out of her reverie. She fixed a smile on her face and scooted around the counter to let her in. Her friend wasn't fooled.

"Are you crying? What's wrong?" Penny frowned. "Are you overwhelmed by all this?"

Frankie surveyed the café, taking it all in before her gaze finally rested on Penny. There was construction to complete, orders to figure out, and a lot of work to be done before the grand reopening. But she didn't feel overwhelmed. She had her passion and she had her friends. One prayer had gone unanswered, but she had plenty of gifts for which to be thankful. She shook her head and suddenly she no longer had to force her smile.

"I'm…grateful for this fresh start. Let's get to it." She paused and held up a finger. "But first, let's have a cup of coffee."

CHAPTER EIGHTEEN

On Christmas Eve, Lily stood at the butcher-block-top island in her mother's kitchen, cutting up a cucumber for the tossed salad. She took extra care to not chop in time to the cheerful music playing through the house's smart speaker system. That would be holly-jolly behavior. She wasn't keeping time—she was simply completing a task. It was pure defiance. She didn't want to be in the Christmas spirit. She was going to have to hold the line pretty damn hard since the house was about to be full of family jingling all the way. The Lancasters did not half-ass holidays.

"Honey, do you want me to take over for you so you can go get dressed for the party?" Her mom bustled into the kitchen, wiping her hands on her holly-print apron, and disdainfully eyed Lily's skinny jeans and over-sized gray cable-knit sweater. "The Judahs will be here any minute."

The knife dropped from Lily's hand and clattered against the wooden surface of the countertop. "The Judahs are coming?"

"Of course the Judahs are coming." Her mom arranged cookies on a Santa tray. "The Judahs come every year. Did you think I wouldn't invite them because you and Brayden had a fake breakup of your fake relationship?" Her mom was never one to beat around the bush.

Sighing, Lily threw the cukes on top of the salad as her mom checked on the contents of the oven. Her graying hair was pulled back in knot at the base of her neck and even though she was rushing around getting a meal ready for nearly twenty people, she looked completely put together. She didn't know how her mom did it. Lily could barely manage her own life much less take care of a spouse, children, grandchildren, and extended family. "No, it's just that I haven't talked to him since we've been back in Bell Buckle and I'm not sure I'm ready to."

Her mom wasn't having it. She stopped in the middle of pulling the trifle from the fridge, balled her fists on her hips and glared across the room. "That is ridiculous. You and Brayden have been friends forever. Besides, it's Christmas—the season for giving and also *for*giving. So if you think you're going to hide out in here all night sulking, you've got another think coming." She yanked a dish towel from the countertop and waved it in Lily's direction. "Go on, get."

Lily abandoned salad duty and slunk out into the living room where her sister's family was arranging gifts under the eight-foot-tall Douglas fir.

"Look, Aunt Lily!" Cadee squealed with delight. "Daddy and Grampa put the angel up on top of the tree!"

Lily's dad stood with his hands in his pockets and beamed. After the way the men had struggled to get the giant tree inside they deserved all the accolades they got.

"It's beautiful." Lily admired the tree while Cadee slipped her little hand into hers. "My favorite part of this tree is that snowman right there." Lily pointed their clasped hands in the direction of a handmade ornament that hung on a low branch.

"I made that one!"

"You did?" Lily feigned surprise and pulled her niece in for a one-armed hug before retreating to the window seat on the far side of the room. Cadee followed right behind and climbed into her lap. Apparently Aunt Lily was going to be part of the family Christmas celebration whether she wanted to or not. Lily would've been perfectly content to fade into the background of the soirée and listen to Cadee chatter on regarding her feelings about each of Santa's reindeer, but the moment the Judahs walked through the front door she knew that wasn't going to happen.

Brayden was both festive and smart in his matching Christmas print vest and bow tie paired with a crisp white oxford shirt. He made a beeline for Lily the moment he spotted her hiding in the corner. The festive attire was a Brayden and Lily tradition at the Lancaster Christmas party, one that Lily had angrily forgone.

"Are you kidding me, Lancaster? Not even an ugly sweater?"

Lily kissed Cadee on the top of her head. "Why don't you go find your brother while I figure out a way to give Uncle Bray the slip."

Cadee called out encouragingly as she ran off, "Give him the slip, Aunt Lily!"

Brayden shifted his posture to block Lily's escape past him. "Not so fast. You and I need to talk."

"Nothing to talk about," she clipped out. "I'm fine."

"Oh, right. So fine." Brayden's mouth hitched up in a sarcastic smirk. "It's Christmas Eve and you're sitting in a corner in a"— he gasped for effect—"plain *gray* sweater. You don't even have a cup of Aunt Jen's eggnog. Something here is very, *very* wrong."

Lily crossed her arms in front of her to look tougher, but she couldn't bear to look Brayden in the eye. "I'm glad it's all still a big joke to you." She'd had enough of his twisted sense of timing and humor. His last surprise appearance had cost her Frankie. She didn't need him ruining her Christmas too. But as she shouldered past him, he grabbed her upper arm and spun her back around.

"Lily, I'm the only one who was a joke." His shoulders slumped and his head dipped with his confession. "I should have never listened to Angela and come out on that stage. Things were going so great at Rodeo Week and all of a sudden it was coming to an end and Angela kept insisting my relationship with you would keep me riding the wave of popularity. I wanted more and more of it. I got greedy." The color that crept into his cheeks matched his bow tie. "Angela told me going on stage with you was best for both of us and you'd be okay with it once you saw that. I really wanted that to be true."

Lily remained unmoved. She didn't want to be moved. She wouldn't be. "And yet it wasn't."

He hung his head. It was the same look he used to get when they were kids and Lily called him out for being an ass. A snapshot of the boy he used to be. Her sweet, funny, kind best friend. "No, it wasn't. I ended up hurting you and I'm sincerely sorry for that."

"Good thing you have your new lady friend to cheer you up." Lily had seen the online articles that had popped up almost immediately after her meeting with Angela. Rodeo Hunk Brayden Judah Beats Heartbreak Out On The Town With Model Sophie Banks. With her anger dissolving she couldn't resist teasing him. "Should I be jealous?"

"You saw that?"

"Everybody saw that." Lily grinned. "Just like Angela planned."

Brayden shoved his hands in his pockets and gave a sheepish shrug. "What can I say? Not everyone's as brave as you are. Maybe someday though." He rocked on his heels and a beat passed before he pulled his phone out of his pocket. "That reminds me, I saw a picture of you too."

Lily's eyes were drawn to the image on his locked screen. The press packet Van had released earlier that week, *Lily Lancaster Comes Out Singing*. "Great headline, right? I love a pun."

She had been styled and the photo op staged, but it had worked. The photos had been picked up by the rags and stories popped up online. And to Lily's surprise, her record sales had held strong. She even had plans to start recording a new album the following month. Right out of the gate Van was rocking it as her new manager. What would happen after that remained to be seen, but Lily had been true to herself, and she was pretty damn proud of that.

"Great rainbow flag sweater, and is that a wallet chain?" He put a hand to his chest to hold in his mock shock. "Angela would hate this one."

"Doesn't matter because I'm under new management."

"I'm so glad you are." He pulled her against his chest in a tight hug. The collar of his shirt tickled Lily's eyebrow and he smelled wonderful, like a mix of soap and freshly cut Christmas tree. After a moment he drew back and eyed her drab gray outfit again. He wrinkled his nose in distaste. "Let's go upstairs and find you something to wear that's a little more merry and bright."

"Boy howdy, you sure have taken *living like a rock star* to a whole new level in here!"

Brayden's cringe alone would have made his point, but his exclamation pushed Lily to see the situation through new eyes. She wasn't expecting company in her bedroom, and with her persistent foul mood since she'd come back home she hadn't done much in the way of house cleaning. Piled-up cardboard boxes lined one wall, strewn clothes covered the hardwood floor, and—she was ashamed when she saw it—an empty pizza box poked out from under the bed.

She grabbed his hand and pulled him into the room, careful to step over the open suitcase she hadn't bothered to unpack. "Don't be mean, Bray. I gave up my apartment right before Thanksgiving and moved all my stuff here to Mom and Dad's, then a few days after that we left for Las Vegas. I guess I better start looking for a new place in Nashville."

"I guess so. You can't go on like this. I'm pretty sure this is a fire hazard." He lifted a straw cowboy hat off the lamp on her bedside table and placed it on his head before picking through the other items covering the table. "Is this a dog collar? Lily, why do you have a dog collar in your bedroom?"

The toe of her boot kicked an empty beer bottle, sending it skittering across the floor and under her vanity. The dog collar from the Clark County Animal Shelter. The gift she had received when she made that donation. That donation she made as an excuse to see Frankie. She had intended to put it on her parent's dog, Parker, but instead she'd kept it as a memento of her time in Las Vegas. The collar was one of the few things she'd retrieved from her suitcase—because it reminded her of Frankie. Her heart squeezed and she blew out a sigh. "It's a long story."

Undeterred by her nonchalance, Brayden's eyes narrowed as he looked closer at the collar. "This is from the animal shelter where Frankie works, isn't it?"

She nodded and plopped down onto the bed, covering her face with her hands. She was able to fix things with Brayden, and fix things with her career, but things with Frankie were a whole different situation. One that Lily couldn't fix.

The mattress dipped as Brayden shuffled clothes on the bed out of the way and sat down beside her. He wrapped his arm around her shoulders and gave her a gentle pat. "You miss her. I know you do. Why don't you just call her? There's no shame in saying you made a mistake and you want to make up for it."

"A mistake is one thing," Lily choked out, "but I really hurt her that night at the concert. I don't know if I can ever make up for that."

"You just said, 'I don't know *if*.' That means there's a possibility you can." Brayden pointed out. "If I know you—and after more than fifteen years of being your BFF I'd certainly say I do—you'll never forgive yourself if you don't find out. Don't carry that *if* around with you forever. Find out."

Lily blew out another long breath and let her arms drop to her sides. Of course Brayden was right. Not knowing if Frankie would give her another chance was killing her. But the fear of rejection was a mighty powerful thing. If she didn't try she couldn't be turned down, and the fantasy of what could be would live on, even if the real thing did not. "I don't know, Bray. What if she doesn't want anything to do with me?"

"Then at least you'll know and you can move on." Suddenly Brayden was some kind of know-it-all relationship guru. But his voice was gentle and kind, and Lily was glad to have him by her side. He handed her the mobile phone from her bedside table. "Call her."

Lily took the phone and flipped it over in her hands, not completely sure she was ready to act. She wanted to talk to Frankie—to hear her voice again, but she was afraid the call wouldn't be well received. What if Frankie hung up on her? What if she didn't hang up but told her to go to hell? Then she wouldn't even have hope. Could she deal with that?

Brayden's hard stare pushed her on. Her finger hovered above the button to connect Frankie's number. She hadn't even thought about what she would say when Frankie picked up. *If* Frankie picked up. There were no guarantees here. At best there was an awkward conversation. A bumbling apology across the miles. Or maybe Frankie had blocked her number and there wouldn't even be a connection. Nope. That would be too harsh. She shook her head and passed the phone back to Brayden. "I can't do it."

"You can try again later." He nodded reassuringly.

"What?" She flinched like she'd been bit by a mosquito. "No. Maybe not later either. I just…calling her is a bad idea. When I last saw Frankie she told me we were over. I don't think a random phone call interrupting her holiday is going to change how she feels about me. It feels wrong. It's not going to work."

"What are you talking about? If you don't try, you'll never get your answer. You have to talk to her. You have to call. No—" He snapped his fingers and hopped up from the bed, spinning around to face her. "You need to go get her. Go back to Vegas and talk to her face-to-face. I'll come with you!"

"Stop right there." Lily squeezed her eyes shut and rubbed her temples. Brayden was working himself up to full steam and she needed to bring him back down to earth. Even if she was considering going to Las Vegas to talk to Frankie in person, Brayden was the last person she needed tagging along. He didn't exactly gain her any points with Frankie the last time they were in town. "That is *not* going to happen."

Brayden's face fell. "You can't just give up. You like her—I *know* you do."

"I'm not saying I'm giving up, but the last time Frankie saw the two of us together you were kissing me on stage in front of everyone. It's not exactly a fact I want to remind her of, so I think it's best if you stay out of it this time."

"This time." Hope flickered across his face. "*This time?* So you're going to go to Las Vegas?"

Go to Las Vegas. It was a bold move. But the more the two of them talked about Frankie, the more Lily longed to see her again. She missed Frankie's happy, bouncy attitude and the sweet way she cared for the kids at the youth center and the animals at the shelter. And she missed the way her hair smelled like citrus and sunshine. Lily hadn't allowed her mind to drift back into the memories of their intimate moments, and now that she had, the thought of being in Frankie's arms again set off a kaleidoscope of butterflies in her belly.

The joyful screeching and fast footsteps downstairs of the kids running through the house snapped Lily out of her reverie. There was a whole houseful of family ready to eat dinner together and celebrate the holidays while she and Brayden remained holed up in her bedroom. There were things she was supposed to be doing. Running off to Vegas suddenly seemed like a silly fantasy. She shook her head as she finally answered, "I want to, but it's Christmas. I can't just leave now."

"Not now," Brayden agreed and stroked his chin thoughtfully. "We need a plan. Do you know what she was doing for the holidays? What is she doing New Year's Eve?"

His question reminded her of that old song, "What Are You Doing New Year's Eve?" The thing was, she didn't know what Frankie's plans were. "I have no idea. I don't even know if she was staying in Vegas for Christmas." But she did know that Frankie would be back three days after Christmas for... "Birthmas!"

"Come again?"

"Birthmas," Lily repeated the nonsense word. When Brayden's face refused to be graced with understanding she explained, "Frankie's group of friends are having a big party at this bar a few days after Christmas to celebrate Mara's birthday. They do it every year—it's a total thing."

Brayden's eyes went wide. "That's it! You can go there and surprise her. Walk in, walk right up to her and say something romantic."

But why just say something romantic when she could *sing* something romantic? "Don't worry, I know exactly what to do."

CHAPTER NINETEEN

It had been less than two weeks since Frankie had decided to buy Café Gato. Christmas Day was over, and now with less than a week before the start of a new year, she was gearing up for the grand reopening of the café and the official start of her new career. The whirlwind of activity with the real estate closing on the shop and the endless string of holiday festivities had been a blessing in the days after Frankie had said goodbye to Lily. Prepping the café for a fresh start was a great distraction and gave her circle of friends a chance to rally around her while still being productive.

Frankie had found her resignation from the animal shelter liberating in many ways, but any of her newfound free time had been quickly sucked up by the glory and trials of being a business owner. The experience was exciting and challenging and satisfying and…scary. But true to their word, her friends had come through, helping out more than just monetarily. That was how they had all ended up in the café just three days after Christmas.

Café Gato had received a modern face-lift while maintaining many of the special touches that made it the comfortable hangout the friends had always enjoyed. Thanks to Penny's connections, the remodeling was completed within days of Frankie formally taking ownership. In many ways it had been a true Christmas miracle that the women accomplished as much as they had in such a timely manner.

Franke's heart warmed at the sight of Hayleigh carefully filling salt and pepper shakers and Jenna sweeping the newly installed wood floor, even if they did pause every few minutes to check out the latest celebrity buzz ticking across the bottom of the television screen mounted in the corner of the shop. Mara was pouring over inventory and Penny was carefully hanging Lauren's framed black and white photographs in an artsy cluster on the wall opposite the coffee counter. It was an all-hands-on-deck kind of day and Frankie wouldn't have it any other way.

She hoisted another box of just-delivered mugs onto the vintage-café counter. To punch up the *gato* theme she had decided to replace the old, brightly colored cups with mugs featuring cat puns. She grinned gleefully at the message on each one as she carefully unwrapped them, but when she got to the one that read "A Purrfect Cup Of Coffee," she actually snort-laughed. Her hand flew up to cover her mouth to hold any other embarrassing noises in. She hadn't laughed like that since the night Lily broke her high heeled shoe at the casino.

That was how it had been going in the past couple weeks since Lily left. It was little moments like that which reminded her yet again of how much she missed what they'd had. The café had been a good distraction but keeping busy hadn't been enough to banish the thoughts of Lily all together. She felt the familiar clench of her heart that always followed those wisps of what could have been.

She shook her head to clear it and set her focus back on the task at hand. The grand reopening celebration was happening on New Year's Day—only four days away. She couldn't afford to get swept up in memories and be led off course. There was still much to be done.

While the service sink behind the counter filled with soapy water, Frankie lined up the new mugs to soak off their sticky labels before they went into the dishwasher. Task by task was the best way for her new-business-owner brain to handle the preparations for Café Gato's big day without becoming overwhelmed.

"Oh my God, you guys. Look at this." Hayleigh had kept one eye trained on the television mounted in the corner of the café the whole time they were working, but now she had grabbed the remote and was pumping up the sound so everybody in the café could get an earful of the entertainment-news show on the screen.

Frankie didn't care much for the programming on the Showbiz Channel since a good deal of it tended to be scripted shows trying to pass as reality television and she wasn't big on celebrity gossip in the first place, but due to Hayleigh's enthusiasm, she glanced up at the television. The familiar face on the monitor caused her to do a double take. It was a replay of an interview Lily had given earlier in the week, and the topic at hand was plastered in a graphic at the bottom of the screen: Country Music Sensation Lily Lancaster Comes Out As Lesbian.

Frankie nearly dropped the "Are You Kitten Me?" mug she was soaking as she scrambled out from behind the counter to focus on the interview.

"I'll be damned." Mara also stopped what she was doing and stood with her hands balled on her hips, staring up at the screen.

"Hush, Mara," Frankie scolded. "I want to hear this."

Lily was radiant in a maroon button-down cuffed at her elbows and her signature choppy blond bob was tousled and sexy, just the way it had been the last time Frankie had held her in her arms. She looked content, beautiful, and…happy. She was smiling confidently at her host as she responded to a question Frankie hadn't caught. "Coming out is something you have to do on your own timetable—on your own terms. For me, that time is now. I recently met someone who taught me a lot about being my authentic self. I don't know if I would be as brave as I feel now without that experience."

"You met someone?" the host gushed as her piercing blue eyes went wide. For a moment Frankie thought she might morph into the heart-eyes emoji. "Is this *someone* your new love interest?"

Frankie's scalp prickled. She didn't want to hear the answer, but she couldn't turn away. Had Lily found someone new already? Her shoes felt like they were made of cement, holding her firmly in place in front of that television screen.

"No, no." Lily shook her head. "She's a very special person, but I think what we went through was a learning moment. It was a life experience I will cherish, but it has accomplished what it was meant to do."

"Frankie, she's talking about you!" Jenna talked right over Lily's next words. She was still holding her broom, having paused midproject to watch the interview. "You've got to do something. Go get her back."

Flying out to Nashville to declare her feelings for Lily and then having the joyful reunion Frankie had secretly hoped for more than once since they had parted sounded like something right out of a rom-com film. Frankie's pulse sped up as her heart got ahead of her brain, but then rationality caught up. "I can't do that." She shook her head, banishing the fantasy. "Every last cent I have is tied up in this place, and we open in less than a week. Even if I thought there was a chance things would work out with Lily, I can't afford to do it, plain and simple."

"Things will totally work out." Hayleigh had the same blissful expression as the interviewer asking about Lily's potential love interest. "She's on the television telling the world about you. At least get on your phone and call her."

A call made much more sense. Hope stirred again in Frankie's chest. Lily had just said she'd met someone special recently. That could be her. But Lily didn't actually say Frankie's name. Suddenly she was chilled with doubt remembering the icepick-to-the-heart moment at Lily's concert when she thought Lily was dedicating a song to her but it turned out to be Brayden receiving the honor. The someone special she mentioned could just as easily be some woman Lily had met since leaving Las Vegas. Frankie choked down the lump rising in her throat. Nope. She was not going to fall for that again.

Frankie grabbed the remote from Hayleigh's hand and clicked off the monitor. "This is ridiculous. You heard Lily, even if she was talking about me, she said it was a life experience. In the past. She's not interested in a reunion. There's no need for me to fly out there or even call her up and act like a fool. She's moving on and so am I. I've got a business to run here." Frankie retreated behind the counter to the soapy water and mugs. She had nothing else to say on the subject. "We've got a lot of work to do here before Mara's Birthmas party tonight, so let's get to it."

As she went back to the mugs, she felt the weight of the others' concerned gazes, but she stubbornly refused to meet them. She had been a fool for love with Lily once and got nothing but heartache for her troubles. She had a new career on which to focus and her friends were counting on her to make good on their investments. She would keep her head down and do her work. Eventually her heart would put itself back together.

CHAPTER TWENTY

Frankie licked the salt from the rim of her second margarita before taking a big gulp. The alcohol seemed to be doing the trick of fortifying her enough to get through a rowdy night at Game of Flats. *Alcohol is my friend.* She mindlessly swirled the last of the liquid around in the glass as her gaze drifted to the packed dance floor. The week between Christmas and New Year's was notorious for partying in Vegas. Flats happily benefited from that merriment.

She wouldn't have gone out at all if it wasn't Mara's birthday. She hadn't been feeling especially festive after seeing that Lily Lancaster interview earlier in the day. But she was doing her best to hang in, even if that meant sitting at the tall cocktail table in the corner and sucking on a lime while her friends boogied down to the band.

Game of Flats had live acts from time to time, and Penny had the okay to hire this particular one for Mara's special occasion. Better Than Sugar was a lesbian rock band, remarkable because their drummer was the lead singer. You didn't see that much. On top of that, the drummer was a total knockout with short, dark, sexy hair and bad-ass tattoos covering both arms. The group played the perfect mix of original songs and covers to keep the crowd on their feet.

She signaled for the server to bring her another margarita as Mara cha-cha'd her way over to the table.

"Why are you sitting in a corner? It's Birthmas!" The barstool screeched against the linoleum floor as Mara pulled up a seat. "This band is great, don't ya think?"

Everyone else in the joint seemed to be under the music's spell, but Frankie hadn't been tempted to join in the dancing. Nonetheless, she couldn't deny the talent of the musicians on the stage. "Nothing but the best when you put Penny in charge."

"So why are you sitting here on the edge of the good time?" Mara frowned. "Come dance. Live a little."

"Maybe after my drink comes." It was a lie, but with any luck Mara would go back to partying and leave her to be miserable alone. Christmas had come and gone in a blur. Frankie hadn't cared. She'd played it off like it was the café that had her preoccupied, but deep down she knew the real issue. Since Lily left, Frankie had felt like she had lost something precious. At first her hurt and anger about the concert had been enough to ward off the emptiness, but eventually that had dissipated. Now anytime she didn't distract her brain with the café grand opening or busied herself with the actual preparation for it, the loneliness crept in and took over. Even in the middle of a lesbian bar while all her friends were celebrating Birthmas. Fighting off her emotions was great for crossing things off her Café Opening to-do list, but it was hell on her heart.

Mara knocked on the table top as if to herald a proclamation. "I'm going to level with you, Frankie. It's my Birthmas and I feel that obligates you to grant me one Birthmas wish."

Here we go. She was about to be guilted into having a good time. She chewed on her thumbnail to stall her surrender. That next margarita couldn't get to the table fast enough. Mara kept her expectant gaze locked firmly on her until she finally gave in from its sheer weight. "Okay, let's hear the wish."

"I want you to tell me the truth." Mara crossed her arms, daring Frankie to deny her. "You're in love with Lily Lancaster, and you miss her terribly, and that's why even though you're the new owner of the fabulous Café Gato and you're currently in attendance at the best Birthmas party ever, you're still sitting here like a bump on a log unable to have any fun. Am I right?"

Frankie's shoulders sank with her next breath. Mara had pretty much nailed it. She didn't know if it was *love*. Could she be in love with Lily after spending less than two weeks together? She sure as hell missed her, and she definitely wished she could find out if there really was something between them. Closing her eyes she nodded her confession. "I think you're right."

Mara let out a *whoop* and slapped the table again before signaling the server to bring her another drink as well. She drained the last of her beer and grinned.

The server set their fresh drinks on the table and as Mara slipped her cash, Frankie squeezed a lime over the ice in her glass. "I'm sorry I don't share the same enthusiasm for my dejected state."

"It's not that." Mara took another healthy swig of beer. "But now that we know the issue we can do something about it. You should text her. Check in. Tell her you miss her."

Showing her hand on first contact seemed a bit much, especially since she had no idea how any contact would be received by Lily. The last time they'd seen each other Frankie hadn't exactly held back her anger. But some connection with Lily would be nice. It could be a steppingstone to more. It was probably the tequila that was spurring on her considering reaching out. If it went horribly wrong, at least she could blame the margaritas. "I guess it couldn't hurt."

"Do it, do it, do it!" Mara chanted as Jenna and Hayleigh joined them at their table.

"What are we cheering for?" Jenna rested her elbows on the high table and leaned in.

"It was more of an encouraging chant than a cheer," Mara corrected. "Frankie's going to text Lily."

"Oh!" Hayleigh's eyes went wide with excitement. "You should do it. If nothing else you'll get some closure."

Frankie's heart sank. It was the *nothing else* that she was afraid of. She stared at her phone and took another sip of her drink. "What the heck. Here goes nothing." She tapped out a quick message while her friends looked on. *Hey, it's Frankie. I was wondering if you might want to talk sometime.*

The group stared at the bright screen, holding their collective breath until the three chat dots appeared below Frankie's message indicating a response was imminent.

"Oh my God, she's typing!" Hayleigh's shriek was full of joy and prompted the others to titter nervously.

But their mirth quickly dried up when the thought bubble disappeared again. The women continued to stare at the screen expectantly until finally it went dark. The message had been ignored on the other end.

"Well." Frankie swallowed hard. She'd played along with Mara's wish and been brave enough to reach out to Lily. She should've expected it would be a fool's errand. She would not cry and be a wet blanket while the group was celebrating Birthmas. "That's that. Let's get back to the party. Who wants to dance?"

Hayleigh put a kind hand on top of Frankie's and gave it a squeeze. Her eyes were full of sympathy that made Frankie choke back another wave of emotion. "Maybe she just—"

With a cheerful chirp the screen of Frankie's phone came to life again. The others stared in silent anticipation as Frankie clicked on the message.

I would like that, but I can't right now. About to go on stage.

"She's just busy!" She almost knocked over her margarita as she grabbed at Hayleigh's hand. *Lily responded and she wanted to talk.* Hope flooded in. Maybe things could work out for the two of them after all. She didn't know if Lily still had feelings for her, but if not, maybe they could be friends. Her heart twisted. That wasn't the outcome Frankie had imagined, but it would at least give her the closure she needed to move on.

Hayleigh seemed to take the text as a very positive development. "I told you!"

Before Mara and Jenna could jump on the celebration train, the drummer from Better Than Sugar addressed the crowd. "Friends, we have one hell of a surprise for you tonight. A very special guest all the way from Nashville, Tennessee. Please welcome Lily Lancaster!"

Her margarita went down the wrong way and Frankie sputtered and coughed. Surely she had misheard. Lily could not be there in Las Vegas on Birthmas.

Mara clapped her on the back. "Holy fuck. It's really her."

Frankie swiped a hand across her mouth, too stunned to care about decorum or do anything other than lock her eyes on the woman walking out onto the stage.

Lily was absolutely stunning in tight, dark-blue jeans and an off-the-shoulder top covered with silver beadwork that shimmered under the stage lights. She strode confidently to the microphone amid cheers from the crowd, but once the band began the introduction to the song, she closed her eyes and shoved her hand through her signature choppy bob as if reining in her thoughts.

Frankie's heart fluttered with joy as Lily opened her eyes and looked directly at her as she started to sing in a low, sexy register.

When the bells all ring and the horns all blow…

Frankie recognized the song as one she had heard before, but she couldn't quite place it. The tune was equal parts hopeful and sexy, and the lyrics strikingly intimate as if they were meant specifically for her. She set her drink on the table and slowly ambled toward the stage, moving as if pulled by a mysterious force. She wove her way through the dancing couples until finally she stood front and center before Lily who was very clearly singing right to her.

What are you doin' New Year's, New Year's Eve?

Frankie swayed along to the music, enchanted by the performance. Around her the crowd and the buzz of the bar went fuzzy. She only had eyes for the beauty on the stage. Lily's gaze remained trained on hers and seemed to beg the question posed in the lyrics. There was kindness and forgiveness and something that looked a lot like love in her eyes. Could there be a future for the two of them together?

As the song ended, applause broke out around her, but Frankie stood frozen in place. Lily hopped down from the stage and took both of her hands. They spoke at the same time.

"You were already here?"

"You wanted to talk?"

They both laughed and Frankie's heart swelled with bravery and joy. Her arms seemed to move by themselves as she pulled Lily in and wrapped her in a hug. She breathed in the familiar cherry-blossom scent, and her brain went a little dizzy. *This is right.*

"I missed you."

Lily squeezed her back. "I missed you more."

Tears slid down Frankie's face, but for the first time in a while they were the happy kind. "I can't believe you're really here in Vegas." She drew back and looked Lily over head to toe to convince herself it wasn't a dream.

"Should I pinch you to prove I'm real?" Lily giggled.

"How about a kiss instead?"

"That sounds better to me, but you haven't answered my question." Lily's eyebrow quirked up expectantly.

"Which question was that?"

Lily tipped her forehead down to press against Frankie's. "What are you doing New Year's Eve?"

Frankie had been planning on going along wherever the rest of her girl gang was spending the night, but suddenly there was only one way she wanted to ring in the new year. "I don't care as long as I'm doing it with you."

"That sounds good to me." Lily's smile lit up her entire face before she leaned in and landed a kiss on Frankie's lips, a kiss that was urgent, knee-shaking, and a definite sign of the good things yet to come.

Lily was happy about her reunion with Frankie, and she was happy to hang out with the others at the Birthmas party, but the two of them being back at Frankie's apartment alone made her heart race with possibility.

She'd had plenty of time since to think about what she would say to Frankie if she had the chance for a fresh start with her. She'd played the scene of how she would make things right over and over in her mind. On the plane earlier that day it struck her that the scenario she had imagined repeatedly was about to play out in real life and she was desperate to have it live up to her fantasy version. By the time she got to mic-check at Game of Flats she'd developed a hardcore case of nerves. It wasn't until Frankie's text—minutes before she walked on stage—that she felt a sense of calm that it could work out okay.

At the bar she and Frankie had easily fallen into their comfortable way of hanging out together, as if nothing had ever happened and their relationship hadn't blown up. But on the ride back to Resting Palms an awkwardness had returned. Missing each other's company was one thing—figuring out if they could pick up the pieces was a whole separate matter.

She made herself at home on the couch while Frankie went to the fridge.

"Do you want something to drink?"

"A water would be great." Lily picked nervously at the fringe on one of the throw pillows beside her as she waited for Frankie to join her. Suddenly all the mental speeches she'd made while imagining this moment seemed silly and trite. She was still grappling for the right words when Frankie sat down beside her and handed off a glass of water. Same ol' Frankie—plastic bottles were a no-no.

"I owe you an apology." Frankie sat her drink on a coaster in front of her and leaned back against the couch cushions. "I know you didn't have the final say in a lot of the decisions about your career, and I know you can't control other peoples' actions. I'm sorry that I got so angry at you. You didn't deserve that."

Frankie was apologizing to her after everything Lily had put her through. *No.* Lily had a wrong she needed to right. This wasn't on Frankie. She followed suit and put her glass down on the coffee table before resting her hand on Frankie's knee. "I could have stood up for myself—for both of us—better than I did. I've struggled with that regret since the night of the concert. I'm sorry I hurt you."

A silence stretched between them, underscored by the hum of the aquarium filter. It seemed like so long ago that Lily had first visited the apartment. Hell, it seemed like a lifetime since Lily had shed her own secret. She was a new woman, no longer shackled by the fear she'd carried around for so long. She was free. It was time to start living again.

"I came here to ask you to give me another chance. I meant it when I asked you to spend New Year's Eve with me and I'd really like it if we could spend longer than just that one night together. I want a total do-over. This time no secrets and no fake acts. Just the two of us being our genuine selves, together."

A total do-over. Frankie studied Lily's beautiful, earnest face. When the country star had appeared on stage at the bar it had been a shock. As much as she'd wanted to be with Lily again—to slide right back into the familiar comfort of her—there was still a small voice in the back of her brain reminding her to proceed with caution. But during the time they spent together at the party Frankie noticed several changes in Lily. Sure there were small things, like the colors of the rainbow guitar strap and her pride flag belt buckle, but there was something…more.

Lily had always appeared confident and powerful on stage, but now she had a certain peace about her that said she knew who she was and how sure she was of it. It showed in the way she unashamedly sang that song directly to Frankie as well as the way she'd proudly held onto her as they walked along the Strip after leaving Game of Flats earlier that night. This really was a new Lily Lancaster and Frankie didn't want to waste another minute without her.

She stared into Lily's big, blue eyes and gently ran her fingertips along her jawline. Lily had never looked as beautiful to her as she did in that moment of raw honesty. "Just the two of us being our genuine selves together is all I've wanted from the very first moment I met you." She blinked back joyful tears as she witnessed relief flood Lily's face. "And I would very much love a total do-over."

Neither needed to say another word on the matter. Instead they sealed the deal with a kiss that held the promise of hope and honesty and discovery…together.

ONE WEEK LATER

Frankie adjusted the picture frame on her office desk one last time trying to get perfect placement. Without piles of administrative paperwork cluttering the place she found she had more space for things that brought her joy like the photo Lauren had taken earlier in the week of the whole group in front of the newly renovated Café Gato. The friends smiled and squinted into the bright sunlight. She sat back in her chair and braced herself against the wave of emotion. Her heart was full of so many things—pride, friendship, love.

She promised herself she wouldn't cry, not even joyful tears. It was the grand reopening of Café Gato, and though Frankie had slipped away to gather her thoughts, the shop was already full with well-wishers. Lily was staying in Vegas to record her new album. Once it was complete she would return to Bell Buckle and pack her belongings before settling in Vegas for good. But even she had taken a break from her rigid recording schedule to spend the day celebrating. A soft rapping on the office door saved Frankie from her thoughts.

"Frankie, we're all here," Lily said as she led the rest of the group into the room.

Mara, Penny, Jenna, Hayleigh, Victoria, and Lauren all filed in behind Lily and circled around Frankie's desk.

Frankie stood and took her girlfriend's hand which started a chain reaction of each woman taking hold of the next until the circle was complete. She took a deep breath as her gaze swept the group. "We've come a long way since the day Mara and I first met here at the café. We've done it all here—dates, parties, fundraisers. Heck, remember the time we even talked Maeve into hosting Drag Bingo here?"

Penny rolled her eyes. "Who could forget? Zig's expression when the show started was priceless!"

"But by the end of the night, even he joined in when the dancing started," Mara pointed out.

"With that damn hot-pink feather boa wrapped around him," Jenna added and the women all laughed along.

Frankie continued, "I couldn't let this place go—it's meant too much to us over the years. I love Café Gato like it's one of us, and I love all of you too." There was that rising wave of emotion again. She swallowed hard. "I couldn't have done this without you. You helped me take a plan into reality. You helped me find my passion. So I just wanted to take this moment to say thank you. The Café Gato will always be our place."

The women broke out in cheers and more than one swiped at tears on their lashes. Frankie's chest swelled with pride and she pulled Lily in for a long, deep kiss.

"Hey, Frankie." Mara tapped her on the shoulder, ending the lip lock. "You've got a café full of people waiting to celebrate with you. Are you gonna join the party, or should I tell them you're too busy playing Seven Minutes in Heaven in your office?"

Frankie pressed her lips into a grimace and squinted at her friend. "Very funny, Mara. Okay, let's party!"

Another cheer went up from the women as they headed back out to the café, but Frankie grabbed Lily and held her back.

"What's wrong, babe?" Lily searched her face before a smile took over her concerned expression. "Wait, do you want to kiss some more?"

Frankie giggled. "I do, but I think we better wait until after the party." She hoped her heavy gaze conveyed just how much she wanted those after-party kisses.

Lily's eyelashes fluttered, returning an equally lustful look. "I'll be looking forward to it."

"Good. Because I love you, Lily."

"I love you too."

Frankie stole one last quick smooch and grinned at her girlfriend. She had a new business, good friends, and the woman she adored by her side. No more low-key—this was full-on love. Her life felt complete to the point of bursting. She grabbed on to Lily, opened the office door, and hand in hand they stepped out to their next big adventure together.

Bella Books, Inc.

Women. Books. Even Better Together.

P.O. Box 10543
Tallahassee, FL 32302

Phone: 800-729-4992
www.bellabooks.com